THE NAVY SEAL'S E-MAIL ORDER BRIDE

CORA SETON

The Navy SEAL's E-Mail Order Bride

Print Edition
ISBN: 9781927036662

Published by One Acre Press

CHAPTER ONE

"BOYS," LIEUTENANT COMMANDER Mason Hall said, "we're going home."

He sat back in his folding chair and waited for a reaction from his brothers. The recreation hall at Bagram Airfield was as busy as always with men hunched over laptops, watching the widescreen television, or lounging in groups of three or four shooting the breeze. His brothers—three tall, broad shouldered men in uniform—stared back at him from his computer screen, the feeds from their four-way video conversation all relaying a similar reaction to his words.

Utter confusion.

"Home?" Austin was the first to speak. A Special Forces officer just a year younger than Mason, he was currently in Kabul.

"Home," Mason confirmed. "I got a letter from Great Aunt Heloise. Uncle Zeke passed away over the weekend without designating an heir. That means the ranch reverts back to her. She thinks we'll do a better job running it than Darren will." Darren, their first cousin, wasn't known for his responsible behavior and he hated ranching. Mason, on the other hand, loved it. He had missed the ranch, the cattle, the Montana sky and his family's home ever since they'd left it twelve years ago.

"She's giving Crescent Hall to us?" That was Zane, Austin's twin, a Marine currently in Kandahar. The excitement in his tone told Mason all he needed to know—Zane stilled loved the old place as much as he did. When Mason had gotten Heloise's letter, he'd had to read it more than once before he believed it. The Hall would belong to them once more—when he'd thought they'd lost it for good. Suddenly he'd felt like he could breathe fully again after so many years of holding in his anger and frustration over his uncle's behavior. The timing was perfect, too. He was due to ship stateside any day now. By April he'd be a civilian again.

Except it wasn't as easy as all that. Mason took a deep breath. "There are a few conditions."

Colt, his youngest brother, snorted. "Of course—we're talking about Heloise, aren't we? What's she up to this time?" He was an Air Force combat controller who had served both in Afghanistan and as part of the relief effort a few years back after the massive earthquake which devastated Haiti. He was currently back on United States soil in Florida, training with his unit.

Mason knew what he meant. Calling Heloise eccentric would be an understatement. In her eighties, she had definite opinions and brooked no opposition to her plans and schemes. She meant well, but as his father had always said, she was capable of leaving a swath of destruction in family affairs that rivaled Sherman's march to Atlanta.

"The first condition is that we have to stock the ranch with one hundred pair of cattle within twelve months of taking possession."

"We should be able to do that," Austin said.

"It's going to take some doing to get that ranch up and running again," Zane countered. "Zeke was already letting the place go years ago."

"You have something better to do than fix the place up when you get out?" Mason asked him. He hoped Zane understood the real question: was he in or out?

"I'm in; I'm just saying," Zane said.

Mason suppressed a smile. Zane always knew what he was thinking.

"Good luck with all that," Colt said.

"Thanks," Mason told him. He'd anticipated that inheriting the Hall wouldn't change Colt's mind about staying in the Air Force. He focused on the other two who were both already in the process of winding down their military careers. "If we're going to do this, it'll take a commitment. We're going to have to pool our funds and put our shoulders to the wheel for as long as it takes. Are you up for that?"

"I'll join you there as soon as I'm able to in June," Austin said. "It'll just be like another year in the service. I can handle that."

"I already said I'm in," Zane said. "I'll have boots on the ground in September."

Here's where it got tricky. "There's just one other thing," Mason said. "Aunt Heloise has one more requirement of each of us."

"What's that?" Austin asked when he didn't go on.

"She's worried about the lack of heirs on our side of the family. Darren has children. We don't."

"Plenty of time for that," Zane said. "We're still young, right?"

"Not according to Heloise." Mason decided to get it over and done with. "She's decided that in order for us to inherit the Hall free and clear, we each have to be married within the year. One of us has to have a child."

Stunned silence met this announcement until Colt started to laugh. "Staying in the Air Force doesn't look so bad now, does it?"

"That means you, too," Mason said.

"What? Hold up, now." Colt was startled into soberness. "I won't even live on the ranch. Why do I have to get hitched?"

"Because Heloise says it's time to stop screwing around. And she controls the land. And you know Heloise."

"How are we going to get around that?" Austin asked.

"We're not." Mason got right to the point. "We're going to find ourselves some women and we're going to marry them."

"In Afghanistan?" Zane's tone made it clear what

he thought about that idea.

Tension tightened Mason's jaw. He'd known this was going to be a messy conversation. "Online. I created an online personal ad for all of us. Each of us has a photo, a description and a reply address. A woman can get in touch with whichever of us she chooses and start a conversation. Just weed through your replies until you find the one you want."

"Are you out of your mind?" Zane peered at him through the video screen.

"I don't see what you're upset about. I'm the one who has to have a child. None of you will be out of the service in time."

"Wait a minute—I thought you just got the letter from Heloise." As usual, Austin zeroed in on the inconsistency.

"The letter came about a week ago. I didn't want to get anyone's hopes up until I checked a few things out." Mason shifted in his seat. "Heloise said the place is in rougher shape than we thought. Sounds like Zeke sold off the last of his cattle last year. We're going to have to start from scratch, and we're going to have to move fast to meet her deadline—on both counts. I did all the leg work on the online ad. All you need to do is read some e-mails, look at some photos and pick one. How hard can that be?"

"I'm beginning to think there's a reason you've been single all these years, Straightshot," Austin said. Mason winced at the use of his nickname. The men in his unit had christened him with it during his early days in the service, but as Colt said when his brothers had first heard about it, it made perfect sense. The name had little to do with his accuracy with a rifle, and everything to do with his tendency to find the shortest route from here to done on any mission he was tasked with. Regardless of what obstacles stood in his way.

Colt snickered. "Told you two it was safer to stay in the military. Mason's Matchmaking Service. It has a ring to it. I guess you've found yourself a new career, Mase."

"Stow it." Mason tapped a finger on the table. "Just because I've put the ad up doesn't mean that any of you have to make contact with the women who write you. If it doesn't work, it doesn't work. But you need to marry within the year. If you don't find a wife for yourself, I'll find one for you."

"He would, too," Austin said to the others. "You know he would."

"When does the ad go live?" Zane asked.

"It went live five days ago. You've each got several hundred responses so far. I'll forward them to you as soon as we break the call."

Austin must have leaned toward his webcam because suddenly he filled the screen. "Several hundred?"

"That's right."

Colt's laughter rang out over the line.

"Don't know what you're finding so funny, Colton," Mason said in his best imitation of their late father's voice. "You've got several hundred responses, too."

"What? I told you I was staying…"

"Read through them and answer all the likely ones. I'll be in touch in a few days to check your progress." Mason cut the call.

REGAN ANDERSON WANTED a baby. Right now. Not five years from now. Not even next year.

Right now.

And since she'd just quit her stuffy loan officer job, moved out of her overpriced one bedroom New York City apartment, and completed all her preliminary appointments, she was going to get one via the modern technology of artificial insemination.

As she raced up the three flights of steps to her tiny new studio, she took the pins out of her severe updo and let her thick, auburn hair swirl around her shoulders. By the time she reached the door, she was breathing hard. Inside, she shut and locked it behind her, tossed her briefcase and blazer on the bed which took up the lion's share of the living space, and kicked off her high heels. Her blouse and pencil skirt came next, and thirty seconds later she was down to her skivvies.

Thank God.

She was done with Town and Country Bank. Done with originating loans for people who would scrape and slave away for the next thirty years just to cling to a lousy flat near a subway stop. She was done, done, done being a cog in the wheel of a financial system she couldn't stand to be a part of anymore.

She was starting a new business. Starting a new life.

And she was starting a family, too.

Alone.

After years of looking for Mr. Right, she'd decided he simply didn't exist in New York City. So after several medical exams and consultations, she had scheduled her first round of artificial insemination for the end of April. She couldn't wait.

Meanwhile, she'd throw herself into the task of building her consulting business. She would make it her job to help non-profits assist regular people start new stores and services, buy homes that made sense, and manage their money so that they could get ahead. It might not be as lucrative as being a loan officer, but at least she'd be able to sleep at night.

She wasn't going to think about any of that right now, though. She'd survived her last day at work, survived her exit interview, survived her boss, Jack Richey, pretending to care that she was leaving. Now she was giving herself the weekend off. No work, no nothing—just forty-eight hours of rest and relaxation.

Having grabbed takeout from her favorite Thai restaurant on the way home, Regan spooned it out onto a plate and carried it to her bed. Lined with pillows, it doubled as her couch during waking hours. She sat cross-legged on top of the duvet and savored her food and her freedom. She had bought herself a nice bottle of wine to drink this weekend, figuring it might be her last for an awfully long time. She was all too aware her Chardonnay-sipping days were coming to an end. As soon as her weekend break from reality was over, she planned to spend the next ten months starting her business, while scrimping and saving every penny she could. She would have to move to a bigger apartment right before the baby was born, but given the cost of renting in the city, the temporary downgrade was worth it. She pushed all thoughts of business and the future out of her mind. Rest and relax—that was her job for now.

Two hours and two glasses of wine later, however, rest and relaxation was beginning to feel a lot like loneliness and boredom. In truth, she'd been fighting loneliness for months. She'd broken up with her last boyfriend before Christmas. Here it was March and she was still single. Two of her closest friends had gotten married and moved away in the past twelve months, Laurel to New Hampshire and Rita to New Jersey. They rarely saw each other now and when she'd jokingly mentioned the idea of going ahead and having a child without a husband the last time they'd gotten together, both women had scoffed.

"No way could I have gotten through this pregnancy without Ryan." Laurel ran a hand over her large belly. "I've felt awful the whole time."

"No way I'm going back to work." Rita's baby was six weeks old. "Thank God Alan brings in enough cash to see us through."

Regan decided not to tell them about her plans until the pregnancy was a done deal. She knew what she was getting into—she didn't need them to tell her how hard it might be. If there'd been any way for her to have a baby normally—with a man she loved—she'd have chosen that path in a heartbeat. But there didn't seem to be a man for her to love in New York. Unfortunately, keeping her secret meant it was hard to call either Rita or Laurel just to chat, and she needed someone to chat with tonight. As dusk descended on the city, Regan felt fear for the first time since making her decision to go ahead with having a child.

What if she'd made a mistake? What if her consultancy business failed? What if she became a welfare mother? What if she had to move back home?

When the thoughts and worries circling her mind grew overwhelming, she topped up her wine, opened up her laptop and clicked on a YouTube video of a cat stuck headfirst in a cereal box. Thank goodness she'd hooked up wi-fi the minute she secured the studio. Simultaneously scanning her Facebook feed, she read an update from an acquaintance named Susan who was exhibiting her art in one of the local galleries. She'd have to stop by this weekend.

She watched a couple more videos—the latest installment in a travel series she loved, and one about over-the-top weddings that made her sad. Determined to cheer up, she hopped onto Pinterest and added more images to her nursery pinboard. Sipping her wine, she checked the news, posted a question on the single parents' forum she frequented, checked her e-mail again, and then tapped a finger on the keys, wondering what to do next. The evening stretched out before her, vacant even of the work she normally took home to do over the weekend. She hadn't felt at such loose ends in years.

Pacing her tiny apartment didn't help. Nor did an attempt at unpacking more of her things. She had finished moving in just last night and boxes still lined one wall. She opened one to reveal books, took a look at her limited shelf space and packed them up again. A second box revealed her collection of vintage fans. No room for them here, either.

She stuck her iTouch into a docking station and turned up some tunes, then drained her glass, poured herself another, and flopped onto her bed. The wine was beginning to take effect—giving her a nice, soft, fuzzy feeling. It hadn't done away with her loneliness, but when she turned back to Facebook on her laptop, the images and YouTube links seemed funnier this time.

Heartened, she scrolled further down her feed until she spotted another post one of her friends had shared. It was an image of a handsome man standing ramrod straight in combat fatigues. *Hello*. He was cute. In fact, he looked like exactly the kind of man she'd always hoped she'd meet. He wasn't thin and arrogant like the up-and-coming Wall Street crowd, or paunchy and cynical like the upper-management men who hung around the bars near work. Instead he looked healthy, muscle-bound, clear-sighted, and vital. What was the post about? She clicked the link underneath it. Maybe there'd be more fantasy-fodder like this man wherever it took her.

There *was* more fantasy fodder. Regan wriggled happily. She had landed on a page that showcased four men. Brothers, she saw, looking more closely—two of them identical twins. Each one seemed to represent a different branch of the United States military. Were they models? Was this some kind of recruitment ploy?

Practical Wives Wanted read the heading at the top. Regan nearly spit out a sip of her wine. Wives Wanted? Practical ones? She considered the men again, then read more.

Looking for a change? the text went on. *Ready for a real challenge? Join four hardworking, clean living men and help bring our family's ranch back to life.*

Skills required—any or all of the following: Riding, roping, construction, animal care, roofing, farming, market gardening, cooking, cleaning, metalworking, small motor repair…

The list went on and on. Regan bit back at a laugh which quickly dissolved into giggles. Small engine repair? How very romantic. Was this supposed to be satire or was it real? It was certainly one of the most intriguing things she'd seen online in a long, long time.

Must be willing to commit to a man and the project. No weekends/no holidays/no sick days. Weaklings need not apply.

Regan snorted. It was beginning to sound like an employment ad. Good luck finding a woman to fill those conditions. She'd tried to find a suitable man for years and came up with Erik—the perennial mooch who'd finally admitted just before Christmas that he liked her old Village apartment more than he liked her. That's why she planned to get pregnant all by herself. There wasn't anyone worth marrying in the whole city. Probably the whole state. And if the men were all worthless, the women probably were, too. She reached for her wine without turning from the screen, missed, and nearly knocked over her glass. She tried again, secured the wine, drained the glass a third time and set it down again.

What she would give to find a real partner. Someone strong, both physically and emotionally. An equal in intelligence and heart. A real man.

But those didn't exist.

If you're sick of wasting your time in a dead-end job, tired of tearing things down instead of building something up, or just ready to get your hands dirty with clean, honest work, write and tell us why you'd make a worthy wife for a man who has spent the last decade in uniform.

There wasn't much to laugh at in this paragraph. Regan read it again, then got up and wandered to the kitchen to top up her glass. She'd never seen a singles ad like this one. She could see why it was going viral. If it was real, these men were something special. Who wanted to do clean, honest work these days? What kind of man was selfless enough to serve in the military instead of sponging off their girlfriends? If she'd known there were guys like this in the world, she might not have been so quick to schedule the artificial insemination appointment.

She wouldn't cancel it, though, because these guys

couldn't be for real, and she wasn't waiting another minute to start her family. She had dreamed of having children ever since she was a child herself and organized pretend schools in her backyard for the neighborhood little ones. Babies loved her. Toddlers thought she was the next best thing to teddy bears. Her co-workers at the bank had never appreciated her as much as the average five-year-old did.

Further down the page there were photographs of the ranch the brothers meant to bring back to life. The land was beautiful, if overgrown, but its toppled fences and sagging buildings were a testament to its neglect. The photograph of the main house caught her eye and kept her riveted, though. A large gothic structure, it could be beautiful with the proper care. She could see why these men would dedicate themselves to returning it to its former glory. She tried to imagine what it would be like to live on the ranch with one of them, and immediately her body craved an open sunny sky—the kind you were hard pressed to see in the city. She sunk into the daydream, picturing herself sitting on a back porch sipping lemonade while her cowboy worked and the baby napped. Her husband would have his shirt off while he chopped wood, or mended a fence or whatever it was ranchers did. At the end of the day they'd fall into bed and make love until morning.

Regan sighed. It was a wonderful daydream, but it had no bearing on her life. Disgruntled, she switched over to Netflix and set up a foreign film. She fetched the bottle of wine back to bed with her and leaned against her many pillows. She'd managed to hang her small flatscreen on the opposite wall. In an apartment this tiny, every piece of furniture needed to serve double-duty.

As the movie started, Regan found herself composing messages to the military men in the Wife Wanted ad, in which she described herself as trim and petite, or lithe and strong, or horny and good-enough-looking to do the trick.

An hour later, when the film failed to hold her attention, she grabbed her laptop again. She pulled up the Wife Wanted page and reread it, keeping an eye on the foreign couple on the television screen who alternately argued and kissed.

Crazy what some people did. What was wrong with these men that they needed to advertise for wives instead of going out and meeting them like normal people?

She thought of the online dating sites she'd tried in the past. She'd had some awkward experiences, some horrible first dates, and finally one relationship that lasted for a couple of months before the man was transferred to Tucson and it fizzled out. It hadn't worked for her, but she supposed lots of people found love online these days. They might not advertise directly for spouses, but that was their ultimate intention, right? So maybe this ad wasn't all that unusual.

Most men who posted singles ads weren't as hot as these men were, though. Definitely not the ones she'd met. She poured herself another glass. A small twinge of her conscience told her she'd already had far too much wine for a single night.

To hell with that, Regan thought. As soon as she got pregnant she'd have to stay sober and sane for the next eighteen years. She wouldn't have a husband to trade off with—she'd always be the designated driver, the adult in charge, the sober, wise mother who made sure nothing bad ever happened to her child. Just this one last time she was allowed to blow off steam.

But even as she thought it, a twinge of fear wormed through her belly.

What if she wasn't good enough?

She stood up, strode the two steps to the kitchenette and made herself a bowl of popcorn. She drowned it in butter and salt, returned to the bed in time for the ending credits of the movie, and lined up *Pride and Prejudice* with Colin Firth. Time for comfort food and a comfort movie. *Pride and Prejudice* always did the trick when she felt blue. She checked the Wife Wanted page again on her laptop. If she was going to pick one of the men—which she wasn't—who would she choose?

Mason, the oldest, due to leave the Navy in a matter of weeks, drew her eye first. With his dark crew cut, hard jaw and uncompromising blue eyes he looked like the epitome of a military man. He stated his interests as ranching—of course—history, natural sciences and tactical operations, whatever the hell that was. That left her little more informed than before she'd read it, and she wondered what the man was really like. Did he read the newspaper in bed on Sunday mornings? Did he prefer lasagna or spaghetti? Would he listen to country music in his truck or talk radio? She stared at his photo, willing him to answer.

The next two brothers, Austin and Zane, were less fierce, but looked no less intelligent and determined. Still, they didn't draw her eye the way the way Mason did. Colt, the youngest, was blond with a grin she bet drew women like flies. That one was trouble, and she didn't need trouble.

She read Mason's description again and decided he was the leader of this endeavor. If she was going to pick one, it would be him.

But she wasn't going to pick one. She had given up all that. She'd made a promise to her imaginary child that she would not allow any chaos into its life. No dating until her baby wore a graduation gown, at the very least. She felt another twinge. Was she ready to give up men for nearly two decades? That was a long time.

It's worth it, she told herself. She had no doubt about her desire to be a mother. She had no doubt she'd be a great mom. She was smart, capable and had a good head on her shoulders. She was funny, silly and patient, too. She loved children.

She was just lousy with men.

But that didn't matter anymore. She pushed the laptop aside and returned her attention to *Pride and Prejudice*, quickly falling into an old drinking game she and Laurel had devised one night that required taking a swig of wine each time one of the actresses lifted her eyebrows in polite surprise. When she finished the bottle, she headed to the tiny kitchenette to track down another one, trilling, "Jane! Elizabeth!" at the top of her voice along with Mrs. Bennett in the film. There was no more wine, so she switched to tequila.

By the time Elizabeth Bennett discovered the miracle of Mr. Darcy's palace-sized mansion, and decided she'd been too hasty in turning down his offer of marriage, Regan had decided she too needed to cast off her prejudices and find herself a man. A hot hunk of a military man. She grabbed the laptop, fumbled with the link that would let her leave Mason Hall a message and drafted a brilliant missive worthy of Jane Austen herself.

Dear Lt. Cmdr. Hall,

In her mind she pronounced lieutenant with an "f" like the Brits in the movie onscreen.

It is a truth universally acknowledged, that a single man in possession of a good ranch, must be in want of a wife. Furthermore, it must be self-evident that the wife in question should possess certain qualities numbering amongst them riding, roping, construction, roofing, farming, market gardening, cooking, cleaning, metal-working, animal care, and—most importantly, by Heaven—small motor repair.

Seeing as I am in possession of all these qualities, not to mention many others you can only have left out through unavoidable oversight or sheer obtuseness—such as glassblowing, cheesemaking, towel origami, heraldry, hovercraft piloting, and an uncanny sense of what cats are thinking—I feel almost forced to catapult myself into your purview.

You will see from my photograph that I am most eminently and majestically suitable for your wife.

She inserted a digital photo of her foot.

In fact, one might wonder why such a paragon of virtue such as I should deign to answer such a peculiar advertisement. The truth is, sir, that I long for adventure. To get my hands dirty with clean, hard work. To build something up instead of tearing it down.

In short, you are really hot. I'd like to lick you.

Yours,
Regan Anderson

On screen, Elizabeth Bennett lifted an eyebrow. Regan knocked back another shot of Jose Cuervo and passed out.

CHAPTER TWO

MASON APPROACHED HIS messages from interested women the way he'd approach any chore. Methodically. At first he'd balked just as much as his brothers had about the idea of an online Wife Wanted ad, but as much as he thought about it he couldn't come up with a more practical way to achieve their mission. How else could he and his brothers meet so many eligible women so quickly? How else could they secure possession of the Hall? No way was he going to let it slip away from his family again—the last time had been bad enough.

Mason was eighteen and only months away from graduating high school when his father died of an aneurysm. There'd been no warning. One minute the vital, powerful man was moving cattle from pasture to pasture, the next he was gone. Mason's childhood had ended the same day.

He'd be the first to admit he'd been luckier than most kids up until that time. His family wasn't rich in cash, but they were rich in land and heritage. The Halls had lived at Crescent Hall for over a hundred years. His parents had been hopelessly in love the entire time they were together. He hadn't realized how rare that was until he was older. As a kid he'd just known that the Hall rang with laughter most days, his mother put up with the dirt and fuss four boys kicked up, and it wasn't uncommon to see his Dad pull her into an embrace and waltz her around the kitchen like there was no one else on earth except the two of them.

A cattleman through and through, Aaron Hall loved the physical work. Mason's mother—Julie—was kind, fun-loving, and just as apt to be mucking out a stall as to be doing more housewifely chores. His parents chatted, laughed, teased and loved each other as they worked side by side. More than once he'd seen his father racing across the fields after his mother to scoop her up, twirl her around and give her a resounding kiss.

His father's death had devastated all of them, and when Uncle Ezekiel took the opportunity to grab control over the land—and their house—it had been the last straw. Zeke, as co-owner of the ranch, was within his rights to do so, but that didn't lessen the blow. Julie packed them up and drove them two miserable days to her sister's place in Florida.

They'd never gone back.

But now they would. And if his dream of going home could be resurrected, maybe his dream of finding the kind of wife his mother had always been to his father was possible, too. But what kind of woman would answer an online ad?

Mason was all too aware how people could construct digital personas that had very little to do with who they really were, and he had determined to double-check any woman he became involved with. Being a part of an elite military team had a few perks. He knew just who to call to dig up dirt on people.

As he read through his messages, he quickly realized the women who answered fell into a few neat categories. Women who expected to be paid for their services, women who were lonely for all too obvious reasons, women who were psychos, and a few normal, healthy-looking women he labeled as "maybes", although none of them caught his interest for too long.

He'd scanned well over a hundred e-mails when he opened one from a Regan Anderson to find a very familiar first line:

"It is a truth universally acknowledged…"

Mason snorted, remembering that hideous, old-fashioned novel from his eleventh grade Honors English class. He'd been forced to write a five page essay on *Pride and Prejudice* and he swore that experience left a permanent scar. But his lips twitched at the substitution of *ranch* for *fortune*, and he bit back a laugh at her list of qualities of a superior woman. Obviously this Regan person thought the whole thing a huge joke.

The photo she included revealed a small, shapely foot with a high arch. He scrolled down to see if there was another more inclusive one. Nope. Nothing but a final paragraph stating once again that she was the perfect candidate. And a single sentence that set his body on alert.

In short, you are really hot. I'd like to lick you.

He considered the foot again, wondering why he wasn't consigning this letter straight to the trash. The women in his *maybe* pile had answered the ad carefully and thoughtfully, listing real qualifications and enough of their life histories to show why they'd make him a good wife.

Regan thought he was hilarious.

Maybe that was it. When was the last time anyone had thought he was hilarious? When was the last time anyone had poked this kind of gentle fun at him? As Lieutenant Commander he was respected and feared and held the lives of his men in his hands.

But while he certainly hoped his wife would respect him, he longed for something no one in the military had offered him, something different than the sharp gallows humor he shared with his team—a real connection with room for some fun.

What did this Regan look like? An online search of Google images found too many possibilities to narrow down. Anderson was a very popular last name, even if Regan was unusual. He dashed off a note to a friend and sent along Regan's e-mail address, then continued on reading more of the messages. Barely an hour later, he had his answer. Regan's address, vital statistics and her official photo from her job at Town and Country Bank in New York City.

He gazed at the redhead, whose glossy curls framed a heart shaped face, green eyes and bewitching smile.

She was trying hard to look professional, but there was a hint of humor apparent in her face as if someone behind the photographer was hamming it up to try to widen her smile.

Now this was a woman with spark. Not wife material, exactly, but perhaps a friend worth cultivating, even if only for the sake of some amusement during his last dull days before he shipped home for good.

Dear Ms. Anderson,

Your qualifications are truly astounding, and you may lick me anytime you are in my vicinity.

Since you find my ad so amusing, let me ask you some real questions.

1. Do you like working in a bank?

2. What do you think of cowboys? And the Navy?

3. Could you marry someone you'd never met in person?

Mason

There. See what she did with that.

REGAN WOKE TO the worst headache she'd ever had and the sneaking suspicion that she'd done something last night she was going to regret.

She just wished she could remember what.

A long, hot shower in her tiny bathroom helped a little, as did three tall glasses of cold water, a piece of dry toast, and four hundred milligrams of ibuprofen. By the time she staggered back out to the main room and was confronted by the evidence of her wine and tequila binge, she felt approximately human.

She brought the bottles to the kitchenette, cleaned the wine and shot glasses and straightened her bed before she spotted her laptop, and the rest of her night came crashing back into her memory.

Had she really answered a Wife Wanted ad? While channeling Jane Austen? Drunk on a mixture of wine and tequila? So much for her self-image as an intelligent, mature woman.

She fired up the laptop gingerly, telling herself that even if she had answered the ad, the recipient would surely ignore her.

But there in her inbox was a message from Mason Hall.

Regan winced.

She clicked it open and read his reply, cringing at his reference to licking, and raising her eyebrows in shock at the way he'd obviously tracked her down. Still, the man must have a sense of humor because he hadn't blasted her, or even made fun of her. Instead, he took her e-mail in the spirit in which she'd written it and replied in the same way.

Regan was impressed, despite herself. And intrigued by his response. She was definitely not interested in finding a husband, but she couldn't just leave the poor guy hanging. She'd write one more note. And drop the Jane Austen act.

Dear Mason,

Plain questions deserve plain answers:

1. I am currently unemployed. That should tell you how much I liked my job. (Nice sleuthing by the way. Nothing stalker-ish about it).

2. When I think cowboys, I think passionate sex in haylofts (you ever try that?). When I think Navy boys, I think wide white pants and submarines and… well… the fantasy kind of slips away from me at that point.

3. No. I require at least thirty minutes with a guy before I marry him.

She meant to stop writing here, with a sign-off that let him know she was definitely finished with the conversation, but she couldn't help herself. The strong morning sunshine streaming in her window revealed more clearly than ever how alone she was. Why not chat a little longer with a man who must be lonely, too?

Here are three questions for you:

1. Do you have to give back the uniform when you un-enlist?

2. What's the best part of your job?

3. Do you have a nickname?

Regan

CHAPTER THREE

MASON RECEIVED REGAN'S message mid-morning. He'd woken up early, run ten miles with the other men, put in some time filing paperwork and then gone online. As soon as his messages came up he found himself scanning them for her name. Surprised by his own eagerness, he thought briefly about going through the new responses to his ad in an orderly fashion, from top to bottom.

But he'd already clicked the link to hers before he could consider that notion thoroughly. His chuckles brought a few interested looks from the other men in the room. He knew he wasn't known for his sense of humor, but he liked Regan's wordplay, and her references to haylofts and fantasies piqued his interest in a way the other women's messages hadn't. While he rolled his eyes at her obvious lack of military knowledge—he was commissioned, not enlisted, for one thing, and he was pretty sure that *un-enlist* wasn't even a word—he enjoyed her e-mail far more than any of the others he'd gotten. He had a list of ten women that he meant to answer and begin conversations with.

He decided he'd do that right after he answered Regan.

Dear Regan,

I'll admit I've tested out the hayloft scenario. I prefer a picnic blanket on the banks of the local creek. Less prickly.

I am dismayed by the poor showing the Navy makes in your fantasy life. Perhaps it will help to tell you I'm a SEAL. I wouldn't normally spill the beans on that, but my time here is almost up, and I figure my secret is safe with you. I assure you that I spend much more time hanging out around military bases pumping iron, going for ten mile runs, and training on high tech weaponry—all the time half-naked with my biceps flexed—than I do in white pants. I haven't been on a submarine in years.

To answer your questions:

1. Yes, I get to keep the uniform. If you ask nicely I'll model it for you.

2. The best part of my job is achieving the mission goal with the help of a few men I'd be proud to lay my life down for.

3. I do have a nickname. You'll have to earn that information, though.

Which brings me to my first and only question. Why did you answer my ad? Seems to me you aren't taking my bid to find a wife very seriously.

Mason

He signed off and wondered how long he'd have to wait before she replied. Maybe he should ask her if she cared to instant message instead of using old-fashioned e-mails. He decided he'd wait a little while to do that. He liked the pace of their conversation so far—it allowed him time to formulate careful, teasing answers.

He faced the list of other women he had chosen to correspond with and decided to write a single form letter he could send to each of them to elicit further information.

Dear _____,

Thank you for responding to my personal ad. Here are my answers to some frequently asked questions:

1. I am 6'2" inches tall and weigh 200 pounds. I am muscular. I intend to stay in good shape.

2. The ranch will make a modest income at first. You will need to be thrifty. It will be several years before we can consider a trip to Hawaii, if ever.

3. Cow poop does smell. There will be flies.

He sighed and dropped his head into his hands. It wasn't fair to send a duplicate response to women who'd taken the time to send him individualized letters. He needed to respond to each one personally and ask her tailored questions.

He hit the refresh button to see if Regan had answered his note. Nope.

He checked his watch. One minute and thirty seconds had passed. He opened a note from a woman named Margaret, who had ridden horses since she was ten and knew all about their care and upkeep. "I am not afraid to muck out a stall or mend a fence, although

I have never been around cattle. It is my dream to marry a dependable man and raise a family. I have included my picture and hope you will write back with more information."

Margaret was pretty enough. A slim brunette with an upturned nose and a serious expression. He remembered the glint of humor in Regan's eyes in her professional photo and his lips quirked. He checked his e-mail again and sat up straight when he saw that Regan had answered.

Dear Mason,

Seriously? E-Mail Order Brides? That's what the SEALs of this world have come to?

I think you're the one who isn't serious.

Regan

He typed back quickly:

Dear Regan,

I am serious.

Mason

He sat back in his chair and waited impatiently, tapping his fingers on the arms of his chair.

REGAN READ MASON'S reply and bit her lip, a tendril of desire curling through her stomach. Which was crazy. She wasn't looking for romance, plus she didn't know this guy at all. She was savvy enough to know that people in real life were very different from the sum of their written messages and photographs. What did his voice sound like? How did he move his body? Was he super-serious or lighthearted? She had no way of knowing yet. She shouldn't care.

But for some reason she did.

She considered her answer for a few minutes.

Dear Mason,

I'm worried about you. You're engaging in risky behavior. You play with loaded weapons, throw yourself out of airplanes, put yourself in danger voluntarily and then engage in unsavory online interactions.

Is this a thinly-veiled cry for help?

Regan

His answer came after only a few minutes.

Regan,

I think it's a bigger risk to play life safe all the time. You have to take chances if you want to achieve your goals. Besides, you're not very unsavory.

Would you like a call?

Mason

Ooh, he was feisty, wasn't he? Regan tapped the keyboard a moment. It was exciting to know that somewhere in the world a man was bent over his computer waiting for her answer to his message. She tried to picture him but struggled to imagine a background behind the man in the photograph that was all she had to go on. Where was he? In the United States? South America? The Middle East? Was he sitting in a tent? A temporary building? Or a permanent structure? In a city or desert or on a mountain? She had no idea.

Dear Mason,

For all you know I'm a big, hairy, eighty-two year old man!

Regan

Her phone rang. Regan jumped, then laughed at herself. It wasn't like Mason Hall could call to check up on her. It could be her parents trying to talk her out of quitting her job, though. Her stomach sank at the thought. She hadn't broken the news to them yet about her impending pregnancy, although she had told them about starting a consulting business. When she found her phone, though, she didn't recognize the number.

"Hello?"

"Regan?" It was a man's voice, deep and husky and confident. It couldn't be Mason. There was no way it could be Mason, but somehow she knew without a doubt it was. A spasm of happiness shot through her—a feeling so unexpected and alien it caught her completely off-guard.

"M…Mason?"

A low chuckle sent tingles down her spine. "How'd you know?"

"Where are you?"

"Afghanistan." His voice was amazing. She glanced at the photo she'd made into her desktop background. Mason gazed back at her with his serious eyes.

"You can make phone calls from there?"

"I pulled some strings. So, are you?"

"Am I what?" She bit her lip at the excitement coursing through her body. How could she be so turned on by just a voice? How could such a tenuous connection make her feel so alive?

"A big, hairy, 82-year-old man."

She didn't answer for a moment. She couldn't believe he was on the other end of the line. How did she sound to him? Sexy? Or as squeaky as a preteen at a Justin Bieber concert? She struggled to control her tone. "No. Sorry to disappoint you."

"I'm not disappointed. What are you doing today?"

"I'm not sure."

"You quit your job, right?"

"Yes."

"Do you have a boyfriend?"

"Would I answer your ad if I did?"

"Maybe." There was a pause. "I don't know you yet, do I?"

Yet. Her breath caught. "No boyfriend. Not for a while."

"Why not?"

Wow, he went right to the heart of the matter, didn't he? "I guess I'm picky."

"Or scared."

She frowned. "I'm not scared. I've tried, believe

me. I never met the right guy."

"Or you don't know you have yet."

She didn't know how to answer that. She should tell him right now she wasn't interested in men. Had no intention of dating again for years. If ever.

"Regan? Did I lose you?" His voice was soft but demanding.

"You move awfully fast, don't you?"

"When I see something I like, what's the point in waiting around?"

He kept knocking her off-balance with that sexy, knowing voice. She tried to pull herself together. "Mason?"

"Yeah?"

"You're paying a hell of a lot for this call."

"We could Skype next time," he suggested.

"Okay." She bit her lip. *Okay?* What did she mean, *okay?*

"There will be a next time, won't there?" he asked.

"Yeah."

CHAPTER FOUR

MASON HEARD THE hesitation in her voice. He was glad he'd called Regan although she was right, he was burning through minutes like crazy. But he didn't want to scare her off. Maybe his joke had gone too far.

"What are you afraid of?" he asked in a soft voice.

She was quiet for so long he was afraid she would hang up, but before he could speak again she finally answered. "Taking a chance again. Falling for something that isn't real."

Mason stilled. So she felt it too—that whisper of attraction and desire that kept sizzling through his veins. He kept telling himself that nothing he felt on such short acquaintance could be real—especially since he hadn't talked with her face to face yet—not even through Skype. But he did feel something and it lit him up—made him feel as reckless as a teenager.

"I'm being as real as I can be," he said.

"There's something else."

His heart dipped. She was about to blow him off. "What is it?"

"You were right before—I didn't take your ad seriously. I never thought you'd write back, let alone call me up."

"And?" He could listen to her all day. She had a clear, feminine, sexy voice that hinted at gentleness, compassion and laughter. She was serious now, however.

"I'm not looking to get married. I've got things lined up. I definitely don't plan to leave New York and move to Montana."

His stomach sank. "Why not?"

"My life is here. I've never ridden a horse or even been on a farm, or ranch, or whatever you have. I don't know my way around animals, I've never done any roofing, and what else were you after? Small engine repair? Sorry. No can do."

"Damn. I thought all those qualifications you listed seemed too good to be true."

She chuckled. "I have plans, Mason. And as nice as it is to talk to you, you aren't going to change them. You're wasting your time."

He listened to her little speech with a growing sense of disappointment. If everything she said was true, she was right—it made no sense for him to pick her as a wife. But he was attracted to her. Were they really going to end this before it got started?

No, he wouldn't let that happen. Time to make a tactical retreat. "Okay."

"Okay?" She sounded surprised and a little angry. Mason smiled. She was definitely interested in him, no matter what she said.

"I get it. You have plans and they don't include moving to Montana to marry me. That doesn't mean we can't be friends, though, right? Online friends? Maybe I can help you with your plans."

"Oh, yeah?" She still sounded a little put out. "What do you get out of it?"

"You can help me weed through all these women lining up to become a rancher's wife."

REGAN STRUGGLED TO regain her equilibrium. Not only did Mason not sound put out that she wasn't interested in being his mail order bride, he wanted her to help him sort through the ones who were? As she fought for the words to tell him what an ass he was, she heard his quiet chuckle and realized he was yanking her chain. She guessed she couldn't blame him. She had just blown him off.

Well, two could play this game. "All right," she said. "How many candidates do you have?"

There was a long pause on the other end of the line. "Several hundred," Mason said finally, all traces of laughter gone. "But I've narrowed it down to about ten who fit the criteria."

"Criteria?"

"The ones who aren't crazy or… well… not my type."

"Got it," Regan said. "Is there one that stands out from the crowd—one that your gut tells you to focus on?"

"You mean besides the one I'm speaking to right now?"

Regan closed her eyes, his smooth western drawl tugging at her core again. How did he make such a short sentence sound so sexy? "Yes, besides that one."

Mason sighed. "No."

"Well, we'll have to go about this scientifically."

"Sounds smart," Mason said. "Unfortunately, my time is up. Can I Skype you tomorrow?"

"Yes." Regan's heart sank. She wanted to hold onto his voice for as long as possible. Why had she wrecked the conversation by telling him she wasn't interested? He didn't have to know that—not yet.

"Give me your call name."

She did and he told her when to be ready for him.

"Can't wait to see you tomorrow," he said.

"Me neither." She waited for him to end the call first, unwilling to hang up on him and cut it short. Knowing as soon as she did so she'd be alone again, with an entire day stretching out before her. She heard the soft sound of him breathing on the other end of the line.

"Regan, you there?"

"Yeah."

"We have to hang up."

"I know."

His voice turned soft, the low tones reaching all the way through her. "I don't want to go either, honey. Good-night."

"Good-morning," she said, but he was already gone.

CHAPTER FIVE

★

MASON SPENT THE next twenty-four hours preparing for the arrival of the newly promoted Lieutenant Commander Richard Slater, who would take on his position when Mason left. He tried to push his upcoming conversation with Regan out of his head, but he was only partially successful. When he Skyped with her, he wanted to project the same kind of calm confidence he did when he led his men on a mission. But women were trickier than terrorists, he reflected. At least to him. Because of the nature of his work, his relationships tended to be short-lived. When he was deployed he had his head one hundred percent in the game. Relationships took a back seat, and women ignored tended to become women gone.

Did he have what it took to spend the rest of his life with one woman? Did he have what it took to be the kind of husband his father had been to his mother? A thread of worry wormed its way through his gut. His father had been so laid-back. He rolled with the punches, took what ranch life threw at him and dealt with it. He didn't get angry, didn't get drunk, didn't grouse and complain like Uncle Zeke always had. Mason had never liked to visit the two story house on the perimeter of the property where Zeke and his family had made their home. It stood in stark contrast to the happy, noisy Hall with its inhabitants' sullen silences and vicious fights.

Mason had never been a drunk and he didn't consider himself the kind of man to bear a grudge, but so far he'd passed his adult life for the most part in war zones. He'd forged a bond with the men he'd worked and fought with, but his relationships with women had been few and far between. He'd rather stay single than fail his wife.

But he didn't have that choice, so he'd have to do his best.

The thing he did know was that when he made a commitment he stuck to it. He planned to marry only once, which meant he needed to get this right. Heloise's time demands made things tricky, but he accepted the limitations of this mission the way he accepted them in every other one he'd been on. He'd figure this out, he'd find a wife and he would have a baby with her. Failure wasn't an option.

Could Regan be that wife?

It had bothered him more than he cared to let on when she told him that she wasn't interested in marriage or moving to Montana. He felt he'd handled things well by backing off right away, but even though he meant to do this carefully and consider all the women whose qualifications made them eligible, he still wanted Regan in the running even if she wasn't very qualified at all.

And didn't want to be.

As the clock ticked slowly toward their agreed-upon call time, he found himself searching his mind for topics to discuss. He decided to approach the call the way he would any mission. First he defined the objective: get Regan interested in being on his list of possible wives. How could he get her on that list? By creating interest in her mind—in the ranch and in him.

Mason tried to see the ranch from her angle. She was a city girl, unused to country life and perhaps anxious that her city skills wouldn't translate to such a situation. She said she had plans, which meant she had ambitions. He needed to show her that she could make a difference on the ranch, and that the challenges it presented were ones that would fuel her creativity and require her intelligence to solve.

He could do that.

What about him, though? What would make an independent city girl like Regan be interested in him?

His mind went blank.

REGAN USED THE hours until Mason's call to unpack more of her things, but she found the endeavor frustrating. She already missed having enough room to turn around in. Missed being able to pass from kitchen to living room to bedroom. She had the feeling these four walls would soon feel like a jail cell. She could stand it for eight or so months, though. It made sense to scrimp and save so that she could get a two bedroom apartment when the baby's birth drew near. She hoped her mother and sister would come for a visit and help her decorate and shop for the baby. She couldn't wait to pick out a crib and changing table and dresser. She kept falling in love with different color schemes. The thought of raising a child in an apartment gave her pangs of worry now and then, though. She'd had such an active, outdoors life when she was growing up in the suburbs of Madison. Would she be able to provide something similar for her child?

No. Her baby's life would be different. But that didn't mean it would be worse. On the contrary—growing up in New York City was the most exciting thing in the world.

Wasn't it?

Her conversation with Mason rang through her mind. She'd made it sound like she had so much invested in her life here, but now when she looked around her, she realized something she'd been too busy to see before. All she had to show for her time in the city was a handful of acquaintances, this tiny apartment and the plan to start a business. She lived here because it had been her dream to live in a big city during her college days. She had loved it at first—all the choices it afforded her, so many things to see and do. She'd been less successful in integrating herself into any kind of community here, though. With her closest friends gone and her lesser acquaintances scattering to the four corners of the city, she spent a lot of time doing things, but not very much time being with anyone. The glamor was wearing off. Was she making a mistake not moving near her sister in Connecticut, or returning to Wisconsin where she'd grown up?

Somehow that seemed like admitting defeat—like admitting that the finance career she'd chosen because it promised to be lucrative and high-powered really hadn't delivered. She'd done well for herself, but not well enough to justify putting her real dreams on hold. Life in the city was expensive. A big salary didn't stretch nearly as far as it would somewhere else. She hadn't saved as much as she would have liked. She'd spend a large portion of those savings while she started her business.

Which was okay, she reminded herself, because this was her chance to build something more than a nine-to-five job. Something that connected her to people. She hoped her consulting business would help her make those connections, but now and then she remembered what life was like at home in Wisconsin. How her parents ran into their friends every time they went to the grocery store. How the bank tellers called them by name. How her own childhood had been carefree—how she and her sister had run all over their neighborhood without fear.

Where would her child run and play?

She did her best to push these errant thoughts out of her mind, and checked her e-mail more times than she wanted to admit over the course of the day, but

Mason didn't send any messages. As the hours passed, a new fear crept in. Would he call her? Or would he stand her up? She'd worked herself into such a fever-pitch of anticipation for his call, she'd be disappointed if he didn't.

More than disappointed.

Again, she told herself it was ridiculous to feel interest in a man who was thousands of miles away. A man she didn't intend to pursue. A man who for all she knew could have posted a fake photograph and a fake story. Maybe Mason wasn't even a SEAL. Maybe he was some kid in North Dakota having fun at her expense.

That would be a blow.

Why was she letting herself get tangled up in something that couldn't have any bearing on her life? Why even talk to a man when she'd already decided on a course of action?

What was it she wanted? A last fling? A reminder that she was still young and attractive?

No, she realized sadly, crumpling a dress in her hands that she should have been hanging up. No, what she wanted was to fall in love.

She stood still for a long time, holding the dress, before she returned to her unpacking.

As the time for the video call approached, she tried on different outfits but decided in the end to keep it simple. A feminine cotton blouse and jeans, understated jewelry, very carefully and subtly applied makeup, and her hair just so. She told herself she would do the same for any friend, but she didn't believe it.

She made a stack of boxes for a pedestal for her laptop so that when she spoke to him the camera would be head-on. She didn't want to give him an unflattering view from beneath her chin. She made sure everything in sight of the camera was neat and clean and then paced her small stretch of floor until she heard the bubbling noise that signaled a Skype call.

Regan dashed back to her bed, sat down and clicked to connect the call. It took a moment for the screen to resolve into a moving image of the man whose photograph had first caught her attention. Her heart thumped excitedly. It was Mason. And Mason was… Mason. Not some pimply kid in North Dakota, after all.

Behind him she could see a large, sterile looking room full of computers, and something that looked like a ping pong table. Occasionally men passed by in uniform. Regan blinked. Was that Afghanistan?

"Regan?" Mason said, peering at something on his screen. She realized she hadn't authorized her image to be relayed to him and she did so now. She could barely breathe while she waited for his reaction.

She watched him scan the screen. Saw his sudden grin.

Relief overwhelmed her. He'd seen her and he liked what he saw.

"There you are." His voice wrapped her in threads of desire, just as it had before. God, she was in trouble.

"Here I am," she agreed, pushing the thought aside.

This was just a chat between two friends. "How are you?"

"Good." He looked her over and it was so strange to imagine the distance between them and see him right there all at the same time. "What did you do today?"

"I unpacked some things. I just moved to a studio apartment to save on rent." She shrugged. "I barely have room for anything, so it's slow going. What about you?"

"Paperwork, drill, the usual."

"Where are you exactly?"

He looked around. "This is the recreation hall. It's where I'm at most of the time I'm off-duty. Same with everyone else. There aren't a lot of options here."

"Is it dangerous where you're at?"

He nodded. "Sure. But Bagram Airfield is the safest place for miles."

His easy answer unnerved her—she noticed he said safest, not safe. "How many more days will you be there?"

Her concern elicited another smile. She liked that smile. Mason was definitely handsome and his grin made him more so. "Thirteen. But who's counting?"

"Will you go directly home?"

"Germany first for a day or so to be debriefed. Then a few weeks in Virginia. The discharge process takes time."

He'd probably be out of touch for several days then—maybe more, Regan thought. Then ducked her head in embarrassment. Surely this little flirtation would die out by then. He would pick his brand new mail order wife and she'd get on with getting pregnant. Alone.

"What's wrong?" Mason asked.

"Nothing. This is just… weird."

"Definitely," he said, but he didn't look unnerved at all by the experience. Maybe that was his SEAL training. He probably found himself in strange situations all the time.

"What should we talk about?" she asked.

"I'd like to tell you about my ranch." He leaned back in his chair. "Want to hear about it?"

"Sure." She found she did want to hear about it. Everything about this man fascinated her, from his quiet confidence to the work he did. She'd never dated anyone in the military before. Not that she and Mason were dating.

"It's a large spread and when it's running like it should we can carry more than a hundred pairs."

"Pairs?"

"A pair is a cow and her calf."

"What about the guy cows?"

Mason made a face and she realized she'd made a ranching faux pas. "Guy cows?" he said. "You mean bulls?"

"Sure. Bulls."

"We mostly use artificial insemination these days. Male calves are sold for their meat."

"Oh." She felt a sudden kinship with the cows, deprived of a studly male to help her get pregnant.

Mason was pretty studly.

She squashed that thought.

"The land itself is beautiful. It's south of the town—Chance Creek, Montana. You can see the Absaroka Mountains to the southwest. The creek that gives the town its name cuts through our land. You can swim in it in the summer."

"That sounds nice."

"The ranch is called Crescent Hall, which is a little confusing to newcomers because the main house on the ranch is also called Crescent Hall. I'll send you a photo of it. It's a great house."

"I saw it on your site. Where did the name come from?" She'd done more than see the house on his site—she'd lusted after it. She'd always had a thing for old houses, and the Hall was positively gothic. Her fingers itched to get to work on it. She could spend years lovingly restoring the place—everything authentic to the time period in which it was built. Restoring homes was in her blood. Her grandfather had made his living that way. When she was just a little girl, he'd take her out to his work shed and show her his latest project. He gave her bits and piece of wood, odds and ends of hardware and let her build whatever she wanted using appropriately sized tools and a special small workbench he'd custom built for her.

It had been so long since she'd built anything other than bookshelves. She knew if she was ever let loose on a place like the Hall, she'd come into her own. She wanted that tower room for herself. Or for her baby's nursery.

"It's a combination of our family's cattle brand and our surname. A play on words. Our brand is shaped like a crescent moon with a capital H in it."

"Got it. That's cool, to live in a house that has a name. I've always wanted a place like that." She bit her lip. Darn it, that sounded like a come on.

CHAPTER SIX

GOTCHA, MASON THOUGHT. So she liked the idea of living in a home with a name—a house that had a history to it. Well, Crescent Hall had plenty of history.

"The ranch was first settled by my ancestors in 1841. They lived pretty simply in a log cabin, but by 1880 they'd accumulated some wealth and built the Hall."

"You must be looking forward to going home."

"More than you can know." What else could he tell her that would pique her interest? "My brothers and I grew up there, and we loved working with the cattle—loved everything about it, really, but when my father passed away, my uncle wanted to move his family into the Hall. So my mother moved us to Florida to live with her sister."

"You didn't like that, did you?"

He shook his head. "Those were hard years. My mother struggled with her finances. She missed my father terribly. There wasn't much left over to get us started in life. Austin had already been talking about going into the military. It seemed to me a good way for all of us to become self-supporting."

"Your brothers listened to you?"

"I can be persuasive."

She just bet he could. "Is your mother still alive?"

"Yes—she's still in Florida. How about your parents?"

"Both are alive and working outside Madison in a suburb called Middleton. My dad's a chemical engineer and Mom teaches eighth grade. I visit them once or twice a year and they come here to see me and a Broadway show once a year, too."

"Brothers or sisters?"

"One sister in Connecticut. We see each other several times a year."

Mason was quiet for a moment. "I hope my family sticks closer together." She frowned and he hoped she hadn't taken that as a criticism. "What are your feelings on the matter?"

"I'm not sure. I guess people go where their work takes them, right? You can't expect families to stay in one place."

"Ranching families do. Not always, but often."

She shrugged. "I guess ranching is a whole other world."

Damn it, he'd lost her again.

THEIR LAST EXCHANGE left Regan uncomfortable, since more and more she had begun to realize she felt lonely in the city, so she was relieved when she remembered the questions she'd prepared for Mason. She grabbed the piece of paper she'd jotted them down on.

"I figured out how to help you choose your wife," she said brightly, although the thought of him waltzing off into the sunset with another woman didn't thrill her. Not one bit.

He eyed her warily. "How's that?"

"There are a ton of websites that give advice about what to do before you get married. They all have lists of questions you should talk over with your fiancée before you take your vows. I wrote down some of them. I figured you could ask those women you picked out the questions and learn more about them from their answers."

"Sounds sensible." He didn't look too happy, though. "What are the questions?"

She took a breath, because the first question was one that was very near and dear to her heart. Now she would learn that Mason was utterly wrong for her—just like all the men she'd dated in the city. Like them he'd be far too concerned with his own comfort to want to saddle himself with offspring. She held the paper up. "There are ten of them. The first one is: how many children do you want to have?"

Mason grinned. "Lots of them. As soon as possible. Like… now."

Regan tuned out the rest of his words. Lots of them? As soon as possible? No man in her acquaintance had ever said such a thing. She felt hot and prickly all of a sudden as desire swept through her so strong it took her breath away. This handsome, sexy, mouth-watering man wanted to have children? Lots of them? And here she was just weeks away from getting it on with a turkey baster?

"Wh...what?" she made herself say, aware she'd missed several sentences.

"I said, that's my knee-jerk reaction. When I think it through, though, several things factor in."

"Like what?" She hoped Mason didn't notice the breathy quality of her voice.

"Like the health of my wife, for one thing. Things can go wrong in pregnancies. I don't want my wife to ever be put in danger. The other factor is what we can afford. I don't think you need to be wealthy to have kids, but I want to be able to provide for them."

Regan swallowed past a sudden lump in her throat. These were the answers she'd always wanted to hear from a man. And now it was too late. Almost.

"I'm clear that I want children," he finished up. "And I want to start right away. How about you?"

"Me?" Darn it—she'd practically squeaked.

"Is that a deal-breaker?"

"Um… no."

He cocked his head. "No, what?"

"No… I want kids. Right away. In fact… I'm kind of in a hurry." Her voice trailed off because all she could think about was her artificial insemination appointment.

He leaned on his elbows, coming closer to the screen. "Really?"

Was it her imagination or had her answer interested him? Really interested him. She tingled under his suddenly intense gaze. "Really. I mean… I just didn't think I'd have a husband anytime soon. To do it that way." She wasn't making any sense and she knew it.

Mason didn't seem to mind. "You're talking to a potential husband." Another grin.

"I'm not one of your candidates, you know." Her voice had gone wobbly and she was unable to look away from him.

He met her gaze. "Yeah, you are."

CHAPTER SEVEN

HE'D COME ON too strong, Mason realized when Regan's eyes went wide. He scrambled to regain his footing in the conversation. "Tell me another question."

Regan hesitated for a long moment, then held up the piece of paper and read the next question off her list. She seemed a little shaky. The piece of paper fluttered. He filed that information away for later—having kids was important to Regan. Real important.

Good to know.

"How will you handle money in your marriage? Who is responsible for earning it? Who decides how it's spent?" She looked up at him.

"You answer first this time." Mason thought it was time to let her set the pace—she'd feel more in control.

Regan made a face. She looked overwhelmed and he knew he was to blame. Damn it, that was the last thing he wanted to happen. He was enjoying this conversation more than he'd thought possible. He liked watching Regan's reactions. Liked trying to puzzle out the way she thought.

"This is supposed to be for the women on your list."

"Fine, if you want to pretend you're not on that list, then think of it this way; I can use your answers to compare to theirs. Like a ruler."

She sighed. A tendril of hair brushed her cheek and he wished he could smooth it away. "Why are you looking at me like that?" Regan said. She looked vulnerable suddenly. And beautiful.

Mason straightened. *Whoops.* He'd been staring. "No reason. What's your answer?"

"Well, I hadn't thought about it before. I guess I would handle the money equally with my partner," she said. "Each month we would add up all the bills and split them in half. Each partner would keep a separate account and handle their personal expenses according to their tastes. We'd agree on big ticket items like vacations, down payments on a house, and so on ahead of time and both save up half the cost. Each person would invest an agreed upon amount of money per year in retirement accounts based on a plan we come up with jointly. That keeps everything simple."

Mason stared at her. "You're kidding, right?"

"No." She stared back at him. "How would you do it?"

"That's the way New Yorkers do it? Everything equal?"

"Sure," she said. "That's what modern couples do."

"Like hell," he said. "That's the stupidest thing I ever heard of." He realized his mistake when she jerked away from the screen. Damn it, she wasn't one of his SEALs—he couldn't talk to her like that. "I mean—that's not the way I would do it." He hoped he didn't lose her over that one. His manners got rusty when he was on tour.

"How would you do it?" Her tone was positively frosty.

Mason knew he had to repair the damage. He thought about his words carefully, wanting them to come from the heart so they'd ring true to Regan. How would he do it? "When I marry a woman we'll throw our lot in together. We're not going to live like roommates. We're going to commit to our relationship—to our family. We'll share our money the way we'll share the ranch work and raising our kids."

"What if your wife wants a trip to the Bahamas and you want a new tractor?" she challenged him.

"We'll sit down and look over our finances together and see which is the best choice."

"What if you don't agree?"

"The numbers will make it clear."

"What if your wife wants something you can't afford?"

He leaned in closer. "I will work my ass off to get my wife everything she wants, but I will also be up front and clear about what she can expect. We won't be millionaires, Regan, but we could be happy." He broke off and the moment stretched out between them. "I mean, whoever she turns out to be, I think my wife and I could make a good life together."

"Maybe you should ask the women on your list all the things they want out of life so you can see if you're on the same page," Regan said.

He looked her square in the eye. "Maybe you better make that list, too."

REGAN THOUGHT OF little else than Mason for the rest of the day as she went for a walk in Central Park and did some grocery shopping on the way home. An image of Mason's ranch played on a loop in her mind—cattle grazing, mountains in the background, their kids playing in the backyard.

Mason holding her close.

With a sigh, she forced herself to picture reality. Her walking down a New York City sidewalk holding her child's hand. *Clutching it.* Eating an ice cream cone. *While homeless people ask for change.* Heading to Central Park to run and play. *Alone, since she couldn't afford more than one child by herself.*

She dropped her purse on the bed to dispel that dispiriting image and fired up her laptop. Mason's face on her screen made her smile, and she was happy to shrug away her reality to participate in a fantasy for a little while longer. She fished the list of needs and wants she'd composed on a park bench out of her pocket and summarized it for him.

Mason,

Financially, I need to feel like I'm making progress each

year. In other words, I need to pay my bills, pay down my mortgage—if and when I get one—and put something aside for retirement.

My wants include a decent wardrobe, my own car, health care, enough cash to furnish my house nicely over time and a fun vacation now and then. I can handle camping trips and state parks most of the time, but I want a few big trips in my lifetime—to Europe, South America and maybe an island or two.

I want children. Four of them. Now.

Regan

She hit send and felt satisfied at how specific she'd been able to get about both her needs and her wants, even if some of those wants were way out of reach. That last bit about four kids was certainly a stretch—a big one—and the idea of a mortgage was laughable, but at least she was able to articulate her dreams. When she had these kinds of conversations previously with other boyfriends, she'd been too shy to be able to express herself so clearly. Was she just getting older or was Mason a better conversationalist?

She had a feeling it was the latter. Mason obviously had strong opinions, and he expressed them as vehemently as any other man did, but she didn't feel Mason would disappear if she said the wrong thing. Mason would never shift from his core values, but he'd also try to find a meeting ground between his opinion and hers. That made him an ideal candidate for a life partner.

But he probably had many qualities that made him less than ideal, she reminded herself. Like the fact he thought he could find a life partner by placing an ad for one.

She began to work on the website for her consulting business. She had a few potential clients lined up already, and it was important for her not to drag her feet if she wanted to have things situated long before her baby arrived. As she tried to pick a color scheme for her site, she lost a minute or two to daydreaming about her baby. Her single baby. Would it be a boy or a girl? She'd always wanted several of both, but of course that didn't matter—at least she'd have one, and she'd enjoy every minute with him or her. They'd visit museums and the park, take in all kinds of cultural events and eat at all the different ethnic restaurants. It would be wonderful.

When that didn't clear a certain wistfulness from her mind, she visited other websites to gather ideas, then browsed through templates. Fifteen minutes later there was no response from Mason to her e-mail, but when she checked next, there was.

Regan,

Four kids? Sounds good.

Once we're married, we'll get right to work on that project. Twins run in the family, but unfortunately there aren't any quadruplets.

I'm impressed with the clarity of your financial needs. Although I have a feeling you and I might price a "decent wardrobe" and "nice furniture" differently, I at least can get a ballpark idea of where you stand. I have to admit I've never had this kind of conversation with a woman. Mostly I stick to dinner and roses.

Ten questions minus two questions leaves eight more. Hit me with another one.

Mason "I Can Provide For You, Honey" Hall

Once we're married? That was presuming a lot, but she'd be lying if she said a thrill hadn't shot through her at reading those words. Mason still considered her in the running for his wife—no matter that she'd never meant to be.

Regan liked his new moniker, even if she did plan to be self-sufficient. Entirely self-sufficient, as it happened. Twins might be fun, but she wasn't after quadruplets. She could be patient when it came to expanding her family.

She rolled her eyes. Her *pretend* family. Her real family would consist of only two people—her and her baby. The way her mind kept slipping into the fantasy Mason was weaving was beginning to alarm her, because it was making clear to her just how much she wanted that fantasy. And she couldn't have it.

Could she?

She answered him right away:

Mason,

Glad to know my wants are within your paygrade, although I thought your plan was for us both to contribute.

Question #3: How often do you expect to have

sex? Where do you draw the line?

Regan (Blushing in New York) Anderson

She didn't have to wait long for an answer this time.

Regan,

Morning, noon and night. Can't think of anything that's off the table as long as there's just the two of us, we're both comfortable, and neither wants to leave in the morning.

Mason

What on earth was she supposed to make of that? She read the note again. The fact that he again referred to the two of them as if this was a done deal made her body hum with anticipation. Was it her imagination or had he begun to woo her for real? The thought left her a little breathless. She wanted to be wooed. She was playing with fire, she knew, but it was too exciting to stop now.

Mason,

I'm afraid I'm a bit more complicated than you. I don't think I can answer this one until I know the man I'm marrying. In a perfect world I would trust him completely and sex would be easy and wonderful all the time. This isn't a perfect world, though. I'm not one of those women who has passionate, angry sex. When I'm angry, I'm just pissed off.

Regan

His answer was swift.

Regan,

How's the makeup sex?

Mason

Mason,

Off the wall.

Regan

Her Skype connection rang, startling her. Checking it, she found that it was Mason and picked up. His image resolved itself on her screen.

"I felt we needed to talk about this one face to face," he said.

Regan touched her hair, belatedly realizing that she hadn't thought about her appearance before she answered his call.

Mason smiled. "You look beautiful."

"Thanks," Regan said ruefully. "I'm not sure what more there is to say, though." Especially since her heart was pounding. This was just a game, right? None of this was real?

"Lots," he said. "For instance, which do you like better, morning or night?"

She suppressed a grin. "Morning. Or night. I don't know." Her cheeks must be scarlet. Was she even having this conversation?

"We'll call that both," Mason said and pretended to write it down.

"What about you?" She was amazed at how easily

she could play this game.

"I'm easy. Although a good long session on a Sunday morning never hurt anyone."

"No, I suppose it didn't." Her cheeks were definitely growing warm. She wasn't prepared for this. Nor was she prepared for the butterflies in her stomach fluttering big time. If Mason was here in her room she'd have a hard time keeping her hands off of him.

"Favorite position?" he asked.

Regan rolled her eyes. "We don't know each other that well."

"Fine, but if we get married, we're going to get to know each other awfully well." He leaned his elbows on the table. "No time like the present."

"You're unbelievable."

Mason shot her a cocky grin. "So I've been told. Now fess up. What position?"

Regan squirmed in her seat. "I like different ones for different things."

"Hmm, that's a cop-out, but I'll give it to you because I feel the same. On top is good for some things, on bottom is good for others."

Regan couldn't help picturing some of the possibilities.

"Have you ever done it outside?" he persisted.

"No. This is the city. There are people everywhere."

"We'll take care of that."

"You're not only unbelievable, you're outrageous, too."

"It's part of the job description. Our first day at the Hall we'll head down to the creek. The sun will shine down on us and the birds will sing and the breeze will blow over your body..."

Regan's body felt like it could use a breeze blowing on it. She was overheating just thinking about that scenario. Mason's T-shirt stretched over a broad chest and his biceps were mesmerizing. The thought of those arms around her—that body close to hers—

"I thought we agreed I wasn't on your candidate list." Time to bring things back to reality.

He stopped fooling around. "I never agreed to that."

"I'm building a consulting business, you know. Here in New York."

He searched her face through the screen. "Regan. I feel something for you. I know we've only met online and on the phone and on Skype, but I definitely feel something. Neither one of us has to make a decision right now but I want to keep talking to you. I want to meet you when I get home."

Regan stilled. "I don't think that's a good idea." Her mouth was dry. He wasn't serious, was he? His home was Montana. They'd never meet in real life.

"I think it's a great idea."

"Do you realize we've known each other less than a week?"

"What's the next question?"

She acknowledged the evasion by raising her eye-brow, but picked up her sheet of paper, willing to be distracted. "How much time will you spend with your in-laws?"

"What are your folks like?"

"Pretty normal," she said, glad for this safer topic of conversation. "Like I said, they both still work. They plan to retire in about five years. They dote on my sister's kids from far away. They'd come to visit us when they could, especially when we started having children. My dad will drive you crazy with his inventions. His motto is, why do something the old way when you can think of a new way that's twice as complicated? My mom will just feed you too much and force you to play—what are you smiling at?"

Mason had been grinning since about halfway through her description. "You said *when we have kids*. I knew you liked me."

"I meant it in a general sense," she protested, but he was right. She had slipped up.

"Your parents sound fine."

"I think they are."

"Well, my father is gone, like I said. My mom is a sweetheart. And my three brothers—well, I hope you'll like them. Like I said, they'll live with us on the ranch."

"In the Hall?"

"We haven't worked that part out yet," he admitted. "Would that bother you?"

"Eight grownups in one house? I don't know. I guess it would be like living in a small apartment building."

"It is a big house."

"How many kitchens does it have?"

"One."

She made a face.

"I guess that could be a problem," Mason admitted.

"Unless one of your brothers marries Julia Child. In which case it'll be great," Regan said.

"Maybe we should go back to that sex question."

She laughed. "I thought you couldn't talk until tomorrow," she reminded him.

"Yeah, I'm going to have to leave in a minute." He checked his watch. "One more question. Real quick."

"Oh, this is a fun one," Regan said, rolling her eyes. "Chores. How would you divide them?"

"Well, that's easy," Mason said, sitting back and lacing his fingers behind his neck. "I do the outdoor ones and you do the inside ones."

"Sexist creep." She mimicked his stance.

"You want to muck out the horse stalls?"

"Not really," she admitted, dropping her arms down again.

"How about this? We buy a case of beer, pack a picnic lunch, drive somewhere lonely where we can see the sunset, pile a bunch of blankets and pillows into the back of my truck and get naked."

"And then sort out the chores?" she asked.

"Well, I was thinking we'd make love, but sure, we can do that, too."

She dropped her head into her hands.

"Sorry, honey," he said, his voice dropping in volume as he bent nearer to the screen. "You're beautiful, you know that? I can't help where my mind goes. We can figure all this stuff out when we need to, don't you think?"

She warmed at his words but reminded herself she wasn't supposed to be on his list of likely wives. "Have you been forwarding these questions to the other women? What are their responses like?"

He shrugged. "I haven't read them."

"Well, there's your homework," Regan said. "Read through all the answers so far and narrow down the ten to five. Then you can tell me about them tomorrow."

"And I suppose you'll ask me more questions."

"Yes. We have five more to go."

"Halfway there," Mason said, "and neither of us has filed for divorce yet."

"That's because we're not getting married."

"Keep telling yourself that." Mason signed off.

CHAPTER EIGHT

"I DON'T THINK this is going to work," Zane said several hours later. All four brothers were online. Austin and Colt were nodding their heads in agreement.

"I narrowed it down to eight," Austin said, "but those are eight women I'd maybe date. Not eight I want to marry. Until I see them I don't see how I'm supposed to pick."

"I'll send you some questions to ask them," Mason said. "You'd be surprised how well it weeds them out."

"What kind of questions?" Zane said. "Like what's their favorite color?"

"No, like how do they want to divide the chores, and how often do they expect you to visit your in-laws."

All three of his brothers went silent. "What the hell kind of questions are those?" Colt said finally. "That sounds boring as all get out."

"They're not boring, they're real," Mason said. "Any yahoo can get married. It takes smarts to stay married. Part of that is really getting to know a woman before you get engaged."

"Know what?" Colt said. "I want to be a part of this even less than I wanted at the start. This isn't the way you find a wife. You find a wife by dating as many women as you can until you find the one you don't want to break up with. You don't plan it all out, you don't sift through e-mails. This is stupid, Mason. Count me out."

"I have to agree with him," Zane said. "It was kind of fun reading through the e-mails at first, thinking about all these women who want to be with me, but then it got creepy. A lot of these women have got real problems."

"So get rid of those," Mason said. "Just focus on the ones that seem like a better match."

"Why are you so into this?" Austin said.

"Because in case you forgot, our inheriting the ranch depends on it. It's easy for you guys—you have a whole year to get married before the deadline hits. I've got to marry someone and get her pregnant just about as soon as I touch down on US soil. That's a bit of pressure. So unlike you cry-babies, I'm taking it seriously. But we're either in this together or we're not. There's no sense in me doing this if you three are going to wimp out. So are you in or out?"

"I'm in," Austin said. "I just don't think this is the way I want to go about it."

"I'm in, too," Zane said, "but I agree with Austin. I'll do it my way."

Mason waited for Colt to speak up.

"Damn it," he grumbled. "I'm still not quitting the Air Force, but I'll do my best. I won't ruin my life to marry, though. If I don't find her the normal way, too bad."

"You've got one year," Mason said.

"I know." Colt's irritation showed in his voice. "And I said I'll try."

"If you fail, you'll leave the rest of us up the creek without a paddle," Austin said.

Colt cut the line.

Regan,

I haven't jumped out of an airplane, rappelled from a cliff, swum through shark-infested waters with a knife between my teeth or blown anything up in over a month. I'm going out of my mind. Send me more questions.

Mason

Regan found the message in her e-mail inbox when she got back from shopping and she poured herself a glass of cold water before she answered it.

Mason,

The next question is about time. Specifically, time off. How much time off do you take and how do you like to spend it?

I like to reserve one weekend day solely for fun, so I try really hard to cram errands, etc, on my lunch hours, at the end of my work days and Saturday mornings.

Unfortunately, I can't always get them done. If I do, I go for walks, or to museums or concerts or sightseeing for the remainder of the weekend. On Sunday nights, I prep for the week to come. How about you?

By the way, aren't you going to be bored on the ranch without airplanes, cliffs, sharks and explosives? Or are there parts of cattle ranching I'm not familiar with?

Regan

Mason's answer came several hours later:

Regan,

I bet there are all kinds of parts to cattle ranching you're not familiar with. We'll remedy that pretty quick.

Free time, huh? Not a concept the US military or cattle think highly of. There is always something to be done on a ranch, and cattle never take the day off, so when you're ranching you have to duck out when you can. On the flip side, you're outside every day and your chores vary enough so that you don't really need time off in quite the same way you do from office work.

I enjoy meals with the whole family around the table. I like driving to town and catching up with friends, whether I see them at the store or at the local watering hole. I like hiking around my property or in the mountains. I like trail riding, of course, camping, that kind of thing. I've never been much of a fisherman, but if you're into it, I suppose I could learn. If you'd like to try something adventurous like skydiving, I'm your man.

Seems to me we'd do a lot of those things together,

but I figure you'll want to throw some more girly activities in the mix once in a while. I can count off a few women about your age on neighboring ranches, and more holding jobs in town, and I think you'd find some friends among them. I don't know what all they get up to in their spare time, but I'm sure you'll figure it out.

One advantage to sharing the ranch with my brothers is that it does allow us to leave once in a while. I can't wait to take you to see Rome.

Mason

Regan liked the idea of going to Rome with Mason. He'd said he was a history buff. She'd have to drag him to Paris, too, since she'd spent all those years studying French.

Mason,

Rome sounds lovely, although anywhere in Europe would be wonderful. I meant to travel sooner, but got so caught up in work I never went.

The ranching lifestyle definitely sounds different from what I'm used to. Don't you ever sleep in?

The next few questions get kind of grim, so let's go through them fast.

1. Addictions: Do you have any? Where do you draw the line with drinking?

2. Abuse: Do you have anger management problems? Do you yell? Are you verbally abusive? Do you hit?

3. Fidelity: How do you define cheating?

Yikes. This is a heavy conversation to have with

someone I've never met.

Regan

Mason Skyped a half hour before their appointed time. Regan was getting changed and almost missed the call. She slid across the apartment's hardwood floor in her haste to reach her laptop in time.

"Hello?" She said before she even clicked to receive the call. She tried again when the image of Mason became clear. "Hello? You're early!"

"Sorry. I don't like these questions so much. Thought we should get them over with."

"Hang on." She searched around the bed and stack of boxes that her laptop sat on until she found the piece of paper with the questions on it. When she sat down again, Mason was grinning ear to ear. "What?"

"Nice cleavage."

Regan looked down, then back at him and realized her mistake. V-neck T-shirt, bending over the laptop to search behind it. "A gentleman would have looked away."

"I'm no gentleman," Mason said. "So, let's get this over with." He propped his elbows on the desk. "One, I drink, but that's it. Once in a while, I drink a lot. I might get loud, I dance better, I'm quicker to take offense, but I'm not a mean drunk, and I don't try to drive myself home. I generally keep things under control. Two, I've never, ever hit a woman and I don't ever intend to start. I don't need to be verbally abusive because I'm damn clear on what I think about things and I'm not afraid to state my opinions. I will respect my wife and I expect that she'll respect me. I expect we'll fight once in a while, but I hope that we'll let it out and get it over with so we can get on to the makeup sex. Three, cheating starts the minute you flirt with another man with the intention of following it up with something physical. I won't stand for it. I won't betray you either." He shrugged and sat back. "This is who I am. No surprises. What about you?"

Regan wasn't sure why she felt nervous. After all, she'd led a fairly upright kind of life. "One, I usually drink in moderation. Glass or two of wine with dinner once or twice a week. I maybe go overboard a couple of times a year—New Year's, that kind of thing. That's when I answer Wife Wanted ads, which leads to Skyping with strangers. Two, I've never hit anyone since I slapped Rachel Winderton in sixth grade."

"What'd she do?" Mason cut in.

"Told Dan Ellis I was on my period. Which I wasn't, by the way. Three, my definition of fidelity matches yours with the addition that I think fooling around online counts, too."

"Fooling around?"

"Flirting, sexting, phone sex, online sex..."

"So you put just as much value on online communications as real time ones."

"Exactly."

He leaned forward. "So what we're doing—you take that seriously?"

Regan felt pinned by his piercing gaze. "Yes," she

admitted.

"Regan, you know you're on my list. You know I want to meet you, don't you?" He looked so serious. There was something about a man in uniform that made you pay attention to him. Mason seemed so together, like he possessed a kind of masculine knowledge that she didn't have access to, and that other men who hadn't shared his experiences didn't have access to either. Would that carry over into the civilian world, or was that simply an illusion the military cast over him? Either way, right now he was a formidable enemy. Every time they spoke she felt her resolve to be sensible slip away a little more.

"My life is here in New York," she said, thinking about her upcoming appointment and the half-completed website.

Mason's jaw tightened. "You're not willing to take a chance on us?"

"This is fun," she said, her voice softening. "Talking to you, writing to you. But I don't see how it can turn into something real. It's not the same as meeting face to face, and even though we can talk about these questions, there are some we haven't agreed on."

"Like what?"

She'd grown so used to seeing Mason's handsome face on her screen. Gotten so used to talking to this intelligent, interesting man. She was going to miss him when this interlude was over.

"Where to live, for example."

Mason nodded. "I did state clearly in the ad that I

was looking for a wife to join me on my ranch," he pointed out.

"I answered that ad as a joke."

"Is it still a joke to you?"

"No, of course not. I mean…" Regan frowned. "Mason, I like you."

"I like you, too. Don't worry so much. This is all going to work out."

"I don't think so."

"Well, I do."

CHAPTER NINE

"WHAT DO YOU mean I'm leaving in three hours?"

"It's all set. Pack your things, Lieutenant Commander, you're going home two weeks early," Sergeant Fitz said an hour later.

"But…"

"No buts. Get your gear together, report to the Commander for a final word and be ready to go at fourteen hundred hours."

"Got it." Mason hurried to the room he shared with three other officers and packed as quickly as he could. There were a number of men he wanted to see before he went and he needed to send Regan a note, too, telling her he wouldn't be available for their conversation tonight. He'd see her soon, though, he thought with a grin. A hell of a lot sooner than she knew. He'd decided not to go straight to Montana after his discharge, after all. Instead he'd take a small detour to New York. He wouldn't tell Regan that, though. He had the feeling if she knew he was coming she'd tangle herself up in obligations rather than take a chance with him.

All he wanted was one dinner—one face to face meeting in the flesh so they could see whether the chemistry they shared now through the Internet could match up with real life.

He thought it could, but he also understood that Regan hadn't ever planned to move to a small town in Montana. She never planned to live on a ranch. It could be a smelly, messy, ugly business. On the other hand, some days on the ranch were beautiful beyond measure. She had to have seen ugly things in New York, too. If she could keep an open mind she could come to love Crescent Hall the way he did.

He hoped.

Soon he intended to know.

He felt like they'd covered more ground in a few days than most couples did in months. He also felt it threw into stark contrast their different opinions on some important matters.

Don't you ever sleep in? she'd asked. The answer was no. Between growing up on a ranch and spending well over a decade in the military, he'd gotten over that habit years ago. It raised an important issue, though. He had no doubt that Regan could work hard. She was obviously quite successful at her job, and it took guts and determination to start her own business. But she was also obviously used to creature comforts. Would she find the ranch too primitive or could she look at it as an adventure? When times got tough would she throw in with the rest of them, or would she hold back, thinking it wasn't her responsibility?

The only thing for it was to bring her to Crescent Hall and show her exactly what she'd be getting into. He made up his mind that was exactly what he'd do.

Heading to the recreation hall to send a quick note to Regan, he was dismayed to find several techs crawling over the bank of computers.

"What's up?" he asked one of them.

"We're offline. We haven't figured out yet if it's an internal problem or something else. We'll have everything up and running again as soon as we can."

Mason tapped his foot impatiently. He didn't want to leave Regan hanging, but he didn't have a lot of time.

"Lieutenant Commander?" a young man said, appearing by his side. Mason struggled to remember his name. Failed.

"Yes?"

"The Commander is waiting to have a word with you, sir."

"All right." A glance told Mason the techs could be busy here for hours. He'd just have to get in touch with Regan as soon as he could.

REGAN LOUNGED BACK against the pillows on her bed, waiting for the bubbling noise that would tell her Mason was ready to Skype. She was ready early this time in a fresh green blouse that set off her hair to perfection. She had one more question to talk to

Mason about, and then they'd be through with them. She wondered if he was communicating with any of the other women on his list and if so, how their answers differed from hers.

Had he Skyped with any of them? She didn't think so, but she cautioned herself that she really knew nothing about this man. He could be lying through his teeth about all kinds of things. Although she didn't think he was. He seemed overly honest, if anything.

He was late today, though. That had never happened before. Mason struck her as a man who put an emphasis on being on time. She hoped nothing was wrong.

Ten minutes later she began to worry in earnest. Had something happened in Afghanistan? She did a quick search online and brought up nothing. He could have simply lost his internet connection, or been called on a mission, although he'd said he was just waiting out the last days before they sent him home.

Regan tried to stay calm. She dealt with other e-mails. Checked her various social media outlets. Even sent a quick note to a friend she hadn't seen in a while. Finally she e-mailed Mason.

Mason,

You're late. Is something up? Hope all is okay.

Regan

A half-hour passed. Then an hour. She found a home makeover show to watch on television. Tried a paperback novel.

By dinner-time she thought she'd lose her mind.

What if it wasn't his internet connection, or that he'd gotten called out on a mission? What if he'd just decided he'd had enough of their little game? She'd told him time and time again she wasn't interested in being his wife, and he'd told her that's what he was looking for.

Maybe he had sent those questions to the other women, and maybe one of them had answered them in a way that intrigued him more than she did. Maybe he was too busy Skyping with her to even remember Regan.

She'd been so sure their connection was real. If she was truthful, she'd hoped it would spill over into their offline lives. She'd wanted to meet him.

She'd wanted to fall in love with him.

Hell, she already had.

CHAPTER TEN

MASON FINALLY WAS able to text Regan when he landed in Munich.

Honey, something's come up. Can't spill the details. Will be out of touch for a couple of weeks.

Regan texted back swiftly.

Thank God you're safe. I was so worried!

Mason winced, knowing if the tables were turned he'd have gone out of his mind.

I'll make it up to you, I swear. Hate that I worried you—such is military life. I'll be thinking of you.

He hesitated, wanting to text something more—wanting to text, *I love you*, but knowing it was much too soon for that. Instead he settled for telling her he'd miss her—a lot. Then he signed off.

In the end, it was nearly three weeks before he could fly to New York City. Mandatory debriefing came first on his way home. Back on base in Virginia there were all the normal jobs to do before he could muster out for the last time. In some ways, the last few weeks had been the hardest of his military career. Knowing it was all ending—that his whole identity was about to change—and having too much time to think about it was a recipe for grim thoughts and self-doubt.

No longer would he be a Navy SEAL. No one could take his experiences away from him, but he wouldn't be part of that elite group anymore—not as an active member, anyway.

He knew some of his exploits would be passed down from SEAL to SEAL in stories. Maybe his nickname would be remembered. He could be proud of the service he'd rendered to his country—proud of the man he'd become while rendering it.

But now he'd just be plain old Mason Hall again. Not Lieutenant Commander. Not Straightshot. Just another cowboy trying to scratch a living off the herds that roamed the Montana ranchland. Who would look to him for orders? Who would care what he did or said?

He knew that Regan was probably wondering at the length of his silence, but he also knew he hadn't been fit to talk to her. Not while he was making the transition home. The smart thing for him to do would be to slip away for another six months and get his head on straight. Heloise's demands didn't leave him that kind of time, though, and he had to admit he was grateful for that. He ached to talk to Regan again. He missed their funny, sexy e-mails and seeing her beautiful smile when they Skyped. He missed her voice on the phone and the way she laughed. He wanted to see her. To touch her.

To be with her.

As soon as he exited the plane at JFK, he turned on his phone and dialed her number. The line rang and rang until her voicemail picked up. "You've reached Regan Anderson. Leave your message at the beep."

"Regan?" he said. "It's me, Mason. Sorry about the disappearing act. It couldn't be helped. I need to talk to you. I'll try again in a few hours. Hope you're okay."

He cut the call and found a car rental agency. He didn't relish the idea of navigating through New York City, but once he'd found Regan and convinced both of them they were right for each other, he intended to bundle her into the rental car and head right back to the airport with her. He had a single goal on this mission: bring Regan home.

Two hours later, he pulled up in front of a nondescript apartment building and confirmed with a sheet of paper that this was the correct address. It took him fifteen more minutes to actually find a parking spot. Then he retraced his steps and called her from outside the front door.

"Mason?" she said when she picked up.

"It's me, honey. You okay?"

"Glad to hear your voice. I was worried." Her voice sounded strained. Well, if she'd gone missing for three weeks, he'd have felt strained, too.

"Something unavoidable came up. Sorry about

that."

"What was it? Or is that classified?"

"No, it isn't classified," Mason said, gazing up at the brick façade of the building. Regan was up there somewhere, and now that the moment had come to meet her, he was as jittery as a new recruit on his first jump. "I was in transit," he said.

"In transit? On your way home?" she said in a rush that warmed him. She sounded excited for him.

"In a manner of speaking," he said. "Listen, I've sent you something special to make up for that missed call. Your doorbell is going to ring in a minute. Can you buzz your delivery in?"

There was a long pause. "What kind of delivery?"

"Something romantic," he assured her, his finger on the buzzer. "You'll like it, I promise."

"How do you even know where I live?"

"Honey, your name, address and phone number are online for anyone to see. This is not the moment to worry about security. I swear."

"I just moved here a month ago. No one has this new address."

"I do."

"Right. And for all I know you're some crazy person delivering a bomb to my apartment."

Mason sighed. "Do you know any of your neighbors?"

"I've met Mrs. Morales across the hall," Regan said after a moment.

"Knock on her door. Tell her you're getting a delivery and for safety's sake you want her to keep her door open. I have no reason to blow up Mrs. Morales." If he'd come all this way and she didn't let him in, he'd have to camp out on her doorstep until she came out.

"Okay," Regan said. "I can do that. What time is the package coming?"

"Right about now," Mason said and pushed the button. A long minute later, the door buzzed and he opened it before Regan could change her mind again. He took the stairs two at a time until he reached the third floor. Checking the numbers on the apartment doors, he found the right direction. Soon he rounded a corner and spotted a slim, young woman with auburn hair and an older woman with thick, dark hair pulled into a knot on top of her head, both leaning out of their open doorways.

"Regan Anderson?" he called out as he approached.

Regan peered at him. Her eyes widened in shock. "Mason?"

He grinned. "You got it!"

"Are you serious? It's you?" She came all the way out of her door as he approached. So did Mrs. Morales.

"You know this man?" she asked Regan. "I thought he was the delivery boy."

Mason didn't stop to set her straight. He didn't stop to say hello.

He swept Regan into his arms and kissed her.

WHEN MASON LET her go, Regan stumbled back

against the door frame. The last three weeks had been nearly unendurable, but his presence here made all her anxiety and heartbreak worthwhile. The tall, broad-shouldered man before her was exactly as she'd dreamed he'd be, but so much more so. He wasn't in uniform, but he was just as handsome in his jeans, a cotton button-down shirt with a dark T-shirt underneath it. He was tall. Really tall. Broad-shouldered. Square-jawed. Masculine in every way.

She'd spent every minute of every day since they'd stopped talking thinking about their conversations and re-reading the e-mails he'd sent her. She had wanted to prove to herself that he was real—and that he cared about her—but she'd found it hard to keep believing as the days went by and he didn't get in touch. Her relief at seeing him brought tears to her eyes. The thought that Mason might not be a part of her life anymore had hurt her worse than she had imagined. She thought she'd been resigned to being a single mom and putting romance off indefinitely.

She wasn't.

And now he'd kissed her. Mason Hall had kissed her. Regan's mouth still tingled from the pressure of his lips. She wanted him to do it again, but at the same time she felt shy and unsure. Mrs. Morales was smiling at them.

"Your boyfriend, he surprised you, didn't he?" she said. "A nice surprise!"

Regan nodded, knowing there was no way she could explain the truth of the matter. "He certainly did surprise me."

"You okay with this?" Mason said, bending closer to her. "I can turn around and leave."

"No! I mean… come on in. It's good to see you. I just… are you really here?"

"I just got out of the military," Mason explained to Mrs. Morales.

Her eyes lit up. "Come over later for dinner. I'll feed you tamales. It's what I do for my nephew whenever he comes home. He's a pilot."

"That sounds terrific," Mason said to her, and Regan relaxed a little. The sensible side of her nature told her it was ridiculous to invite a man she didn't know into her apartment. But Mrs. Morales had seen them together and if anything happened she'd call the police. She opened the door and ushered him in, remembering too late the state of the tiny space.

"Sorry about the mess," she said. "I still haven't figured out where to put everything."

"No problem," he said, taking in the bed, the piled boxes in the corner, the crammed shelves.

"So… were you ever actually in Afghanistan?" she asked, clasping her hands together nervously. She couldn't believe Mason was standing here in the flesh—here in New York.

"Yes, I was," he assured her. "I was supposed to fly out later, but things changed at the last minute. I guess they got tired of me."

"But… why are you here? I thought you would go straight to Montana after you were discharged."

He took her hand. "Because," he said, pulling her closer slowly, this time giving her a chance to pull away, "I couldn't wait one more day to see you." He bent down to kiss her and despite her best intentions, Regan found herself tilting her head to kiss him back. He started gently, but soon the intensity of his kiss grew. He slid his arms around her and pulled her tight against his body. Her hands went of their own volition around his neck. She liked the prickly sensation of his buzz cut under her fingers and loved the feeling of his hands low on her waist. She didn't know how she could have fallen so fast for a man who'd been halfway around the world just a short time ago, but she had.

"Regan," he said when they pulled apart. "God, you're more beautiful than I thought."

Suddenly shy, she pulled away and crossed to the kitchen. "Would you like a drink of something? Water? Pop? I don't have any beer."

"Water's fine," he said, following her. "I haven't scared you, have I? Showing up like this?"

She poured the glass of water. Handed it to him, then leaned back against the counter. "Actually, you have."

Mason stilled. "That's not my intention."

"I know, and it's really good to see you. Really good. The thing is," she paused, searching for the right words. "Something like this can't work out. Us—meeting online. Swapping e-mails, texting, Skyping… that's not the way the world works. What?"

Mason was chuckling. "Actually, it's exactly the way

the world works. Do you know how many times in history something similar has happened? What about the mail order brides who helped settle the west? They established relationships through the written word, just like we did. They exchanged photos and descriptions of themselves. What we're doing is much easier. All they had were letters. We had Skype. So a computer screen separated us when we talked, so what? We still saw each other's faces. We saw each other's reactions. We know each other just as well as the average couple who meets at a party or bar do when they have their first real date."

"I guess so," Regan said. She wanted to be convinced. She just didn't want to be stupid.

"Can we at least spend the afternoon together? Have dinner with Mrs. Morales? She can be our chaperone."

"Okay," Regan said, not giving herself a chance to think it through. "The Morales seem to eat around six. We have several hours until then." Her skin heated as she thought of intimate ways they could pass those hours. That would be far from a wise choice. Still, she wondered what it would be like to explore the body of this handsome man. What would his skin feel like under her hands? What would he do to her? How would he feel inside of her?

She looked away, but Mason must have read her mind again, because he came closer, rested his hands on her hips and said, "I want to kiss you again. You all right with that?"

She nodded. She was more than all right with that. When Mason cupped her face in his hands, she tilted her chin up willingly to meet him halfway. Her heart beat strong and fast as their mouths met. This time he pulled her in closer, asking for more—demanding it. She met him with equal passion and longing, sliding her hands up over his chest. He was so big, so strong. She'd never met a man quite like this before, his muscles hard as steel underneath her fingertips. She felt small, fragile, overwhelmed by the tenderness with which he touched her. She had the feeling he was enjoying his exploration of her—that he was okay with taking it slow. At least for now.

When he pulled back there was a look in his eyes that took her breath away.

He wanted her. And she wanted him right back.

"We'd better get out of here before I overstep my common sense," Mason said. "How about a walk? I could use one to stretch my legs."

"That sounds good," she said gratefully. "Do you want to sight-see or head over to Central Park?"

"Central Park sounds good," he said. "I don't suppose you have a football or Frisbee or something?"

She brightened. "Actually, I do."

CHAPTER ELEVEN

MASON TOOK HER hand as they left her building, and Regan didn't pull away. It was a short ride to the Park and then they joined the other sunshine-seekers out for a stroll on this beautiful April day. Every time she was brave enough to slide a sideways glance Mason's way, she found him looking back at her. His gaze was direct, but not intimidating. She had a feeling he was trying to figure her out in the same way she was trying to understand him. His hand was rough and calloused, his fingers dwarfing hers. It felt right and natural to hold hands with him, though—as if they'd always done this. Did that mean that she'd found someone special? Regan hoped so.

But what if she had? What could it possibly mean? He was going to live in Montana, and she was due to get pregnant in just under a month. Their lives couldn't possibly line up. What would a cowboy want with New York? And what would she want with life on a ranch? The very idea was ridiculous. She'd be as out of place there as diamonds on a pig. As lonely as she'd been in these past few months, wouldn't she be lonelier in

Montana—on a ranch in the middle of nowhere?

Mason interrupted this dark train of thought when he stooped to pick something up from the pavement—a very battered, very dusty stuffed dinosaur, she realized. He scanned the area and honed in on a woman pushing a stroller ahead of them.

"Be back in a minute." He jogged up to the young mother striding down the path in black yoga pants and a lime green jacket. Regan watched her look up in alarm at his approach, take in the dinosaur in his hands and visibly relax. Mason bent down and handed the dinosaur to the toddler in the stroller, who lit up at the sight of his toy and grabbed it with both hands. Both Mason and the mother laughed at his delighted reaction. Regan was close enough to hear her thank him profusely for returning the toy.

"Say thank you to the nice man," she told her son.

"Thank you!" the boy yelled enthusiastically.

Regan let out a long breath, melting at Mason's answering smile for the little boy. He was kind. Considerate. Thoughtful.

A real man.

As he turned, caught sight of her and brightened like the boy when he saw his dinosaur, Regan's heart soared. This man liked her. Liked *her*.

She had the feeling her whole life was about to change.

Maybe Montana wouldn't be so bad after all.

When they arrived at a relatively empty patch of grass, Regan recognized the mistake she had made.

Playing Frisbee meant that Mason was standing far away from her. They could chat while they sent the dayglo orange disc back and forth, but they couldn't touch.

She wanted to touch. But she wanted to keep things light, too.

After sending the disc back and forth a few times, and participating in some stilted conversation, she remembered a game she used to play with her sister when they were young. She leaped up to grab Mason's latest throw and trotted over to him. Taking his hand she tugged him toward a wooded area.

"You want to play Frisbee in the woods?" he asked. "I don't think that's going to work so well."

"I want to play target Frisbee."

"What's that?"

They came to a stop about twenty feet from the trees. Regan pointed to a dangling branch that must have been damaged in a winter storm. "Ten points says I'll hit that." She aimed, flicked her wrist and sent the disc on a rather wobbly trajectory that just managed to hit the tip of the dangling branch. "Ten points!" She went to retrieve the Frisbee. "Your turn."

"I've never heard of this game."

"Are you kidding? Everyone's heard of target Frisbee. It's super big in the military!"

Mason snorted at her fake earnest tone. "I don't think so." But he pointed to a slightly higher branch. "Fifteen points says I hit that." He nailed it.

Regan was impressed, but she wasn't going to show

it. "Anyone could hit that." She grabbed the Frisbee from him when he brought it back and pointed to a branch angling away from them. "Twenty points for that one."

"Give it here—I'll make that shot."

She elbowed him aside. "Wait your turn, sailor. I'll show you how it's done." She was glad to see that Mason could take some kidding around. If he was stiff and formal she wouldn't have liked him at all. She wanted grownup things—marriage, a family—but she didn't want to have to act like a grownup all the time. Life was way too short for that.

Besides, if memory from her teenage years served, sometimes horsing around with a guy you liked could lead to some interesting consequences.

She flung the Frisbee as hard as she could, but this time her shot was wildly off. Mason laughed out loud, then ducked away when she went after him. She gave chase until he stopped short and she smacked into him. Mason reacted so fast she didn't know how she ended up in his arms or pinned on the ground beneath him, but there she was flat on her back, and there he was above her. And if she wasn't mistaken, he was going to kiss her again.

She wasn't mistaken at all.

When he pulled her to her feet a few minutes later, she felt dizzy. "What was that for?"

"You missed a shot. You had to take your penalty." He tugged her along to go retrieve the Frisbee and that's how they played the rest of the game, taking wilder and wilder shots, racking up points for making them, racking up soul-searing kisses when they missed and holding hands each time they retrieved the Frisbee. An hour later, Regan ached with the desire to get even closer to him.

When was the last time she'd had such simple fun? When was the last time she'd been with such a sexy, confident man? Her last boyfriend would have had to make every shot just to prove how competent he was. It would have never occurred to him that it could be fun to lose.

By the time they headed home, their arms around each other's waists, Regan felt like she'd known Mason for months, not hours. It felt so right to touch him, to talk to him—to lean against him, and even to kiss him. She found herself telling him all about coming to New York, longing for the excitement she thought city life would bring, and how it hadn't ended up being all it was cracked up to be.

"What's the best part?" Mason asked her as they walked down the cracked sidewalk to her apartment building.

"The architecture," she said without hesitation. "I'm a sucker for architecture—especially older buildings."

"What's the worst part?"

"The loneliness."

His arm tightened around her waist. "You're not alone anymore."

★ ★ ★

MASON WAS GRATEFUL to have dinner with the Morales. If they'd had dinner by themselves at some romantic restaurant, he probably would have proposed. Regan was all he'd hoped she'd be and more—beautiful, smart, funny, silly. He'd worried some about coming to meet her so soon after coming home. The truth was, it wasn't easy to transition from military to civilian life. At times during the last few weeks he'd felt off-balance, like his reactions weren't in sync with reality. He'd listened to his counselor about what to expect upon reentering society, like coming home from a tour of duty but ten times worse. He'd been prepared to watch his temper and excuse himself if he felt he was veering off course. Since Central Park was a crowded place, he'd cautioned himself that it might not suit him. That maybe it would all be too much.

Regan's game had distracted him from anything else, though and he'd had fun today, plain and simple. What a relief to find he wasn't a ticking time bomb of emotions. Maybe he was better off than most because he had something to look forward to. The return of his family's ranch. The rebuilding of his family's livelihood.

And Regan. Sweet, beautiful Regan.

If he was alone with her, he didn't know how he'd contain himself, so it was a good thing that the Morales family would keep him on track. Regan told him she had gotten to know Annamaria because of the Morales' new baby, Santiago. He was the sweetest infant she'd ever seen and when Annamaria let her hold him she never wanted to give him back.

Mason's heart had warmed to hear how she talked about the baby. Regan was a woman who was ready for love, marriage and family. He now thought he was ready, too. When Heloise's letter had come, the idea of rushing into such an arrangement had stopped him in his tracks, but after today he found that nothing seemed more enticing. Love with Regan. Marriage with Regan. Making babies with her.

Best not to think about that last one right now, however. Mason shifted as they stood in the hall outside the Morales' apartment. The door opened and a stocky, black haired, middle-aged man beamed at them.

"Regan! Come in! Dinner's almost ready."

"Hi Antonio. This is my friend, Mason Hall. Mason, this is Antonio Morales."

He shook hands with the man, accepted his offer of a beer and allowed himself to be led to the living room while Regan joined Annamaria in the kitchen. A minute later she was back.

"She won't let me help." Instead, she went to pick up Santiago from his play pen and sat next to Mason, snuggling the infant in her arms. Santiago gurgled and laughed when she propped him on her lap and rubbed her nose against his. Watching Regan bend over the infant, Mason felt his heart shift in a funny way. He leaned closer, wishing he could put his arm around her shoulders.

"Do you want to hold him?"

Mason hesitated. Hold the baby? He'd never done that before. "I don't know how."

"It's easy." She smiled up at him and transferred Santiago carefully into his arms. Mason held his breath, afraid to hurt the little mite, but the baby wiggled with happiness and wrapped his tiny hand around Mason's thumb.

"He's a strong little guy," he said. Santiago watched him with big, brown eyes.

"Very strong," Antonio agreed with the calm assurance of a proud father.

Regan was watching him too with something like hunger in her eyes. He remembered what she'd said about wanting children. Did he look as good to her holding Santiago as she had looked to him? He sat back with a smile. He'd hold the baby until dinner, in that case.

IF MASON HAD been sexy before, now he was irresistible. The juxtaposition of the baby's tiny body snuggled into his large biceps made Regan tingle all over with desire. Suddenly she didn't care about being sensible. She didn't care about anything except getting closer to Mason. She wanted to be tucked as closely to him as the baby in his arms.

Regan struggled to keep her mind off what would happen after dinner. Mason hadn't mentioned a hotel, and she didn't even know how long he planned to stay. Would he expect to sleep over?

Did she want him to?

The answer was a resounding yes—she did want him to. And at the same time she wanted to be smart. While her body ached to be closer to Mason, she was beginning to think he could be much more than a fling—more than a boyfriend, even. Of course, Mason had been clear since day one he was looking for a wife, but she'd never been clear that she'd been looking for a husband.

Now she thought she might be. And she thought she might have found him.

After they'd eaten and done the dishes, they returned to Regan's apartment with a healthy plateful of leftovers for when they got hungry later, as Annamaria put it. Regan slid it into her refrigerator and joined Mason on the bed.

He tugged her closer. "Regan, I'm going to ask you something and I want you to keep an open mind about it."

She tensed, wondering if he was going to ask to stay the night. She still didn't have an answer, although her body knew exactly what it wanted to do.

"You don't have a job and as far as I can tell you don't have any other obligations right now. It's early in the month and you've paid your rent."

Regan wondered where this was going. So far, he was right, but what did that have to do with spending the night?

"Come home with me." He squeezed her hand. "Come to Crescent Hall for the rest of May. If you hate it, or hate me I'll fly you home and pay for next month's rent, since I'll have kept you from working. If you like it and like me," he smiled down at her, "I'll help you move the rest of your things out to Montana. What do you say?"

All the reasons to say no crowded into her mind at once. She didn't know him. He could be a serial killer. She would get behind on starting her business. She might miss her artificial insemination appointment. No—she thought for a moment—she could arrange things so she'd be back for that.

If things didn't work out with Mason.

Shouldn't she give old-fashioned love and romance one last try? Here was a man who wanted the same things she did—marriage, a family. She hadn't set out to be a single mother. That had been her fall-back plan.

Maybe Mason represented the dream.

"Yes," she said.

"Yes?" Mason looked surprised. She had a feeling he'd been about to launch into a series of well-thought-out arguments. "You mean it?"

She nodded. "Yes." What else could she say? Mason was right—sometimes you couldn't play it safe. Sometimes you had to take what life offered you or risk losing the chance at happiness forever. She couldn't let Mason walk out her door given the way she felt about him. She could either go with him or stay home with her broken heart. She decided to take the risk.

Mason whooped and gathered her into his arms, pulling her right onto his lap. "You won't regret it. I swear." He kissed her until her body thrummed with desire, until she found herself leaning into him, wanting to be closer. "Name your ground rules."

"Ground rules?" Regan repeated, too dazed by the kiss to think straight at the moment. Mason was everything she'd ever wanted in a man. Smart. Strong. And the best kisser she'd ever met.

"It isn't like I picked you up at a bar," Mason said. "Let's not play games. You know I'm looking for a wife. If you come to Montana with me, it will be to decide if you want me to be your husband. I don't want to blow this by stepping over the lines. So tell me straight out." He dropped a kiss on her lips. "Where is the line? Can I kiss you? Can I do more than that?"

She wanted him to do more than that, but she tried to focus on what he was really asking. She appreciated that he cared about her enough to want to be clear. At the same time she wished he would just lay her down and make love to her right now. She wanted to be naked with Mason.

"For now, just kissing," she said. "We don't make love until we're really sure about us. And—" She broke off, afraid to say the next part.

"And?"

"And I have to be back here by May twenty-sixth."

"That's three and a half weeks."

"That's non-negotiable." She used the tone she took at the bank with unruly customers.

Mason groaned but didn't argue. Instead, he cupped the back of her head and pulled her close for another soul-searching kiss. His mouth plundered hers until her entire body blazed with unmet wants. She wrapped her arms around his neck. She wanted to undo the buttons of his shirt and explore more of him, but she knew all too well that once they started down that path there would be no stopping.

She leaned forward to press her breasts against his chest, aching for him to touch them, but he kept his hands resolutely on her waist. A few minutes later, he angled around to lie back on the bed with her on top of him, but despite their intimate position, all they did was make out.

His stubble pricked her and she ran her hands along his jaw, delighting in the feel of it. It was so male, so… him. He was here, she realized all over again. Here, with her.

"What are you thinking?" he asked.

"I'm happy."

"So am I."

CHAPTER TWELVE

MASON DIDN'T THINK he'd ever had such a glorious and simultaneously frustrating night since he took Carrie Fontaine to the eighth grade dance. Nor had he spent so much time making out with a woman since that era, either, especially without taking things further. He'd been so hard through most of it that he'd ached and his hands itched to touch all the places on her body she'd labelled off-limits. He knew Regan was trying to act more responsibly than a teenager, but he would have gladly shucked off their clothes, gone for it and dealt with the consequences later. He'd booked their flights before they went to bed. After they'd talked and kissed for hours, they'd finally slept, but Mason didn't feel rested.

"Tell me more about the ranch." Regan broke into his thoughts. Soon they needed to get up and get packing. For now he relished this time beside her in bed. They'd remained clothed—him in his boxers, Regan in a soft T-shirt and panties—but he'd woken to find her curled against him. He couldn't believe how right it felt.

"I don't want to lie to you. Things are pretty rough there. My uncle owned the ranch for a decade before he died and a few years into it, he kind of gave up. Without my father's help, it was too much for him to handle alone and his son never wanted any part of ranching. The house is in bad shape. We'll need to fix some of the shingles and windows at the very least. It needs a coat of paint, too. I have no idea what we'll find inside. I guess if I was smart I'd have gone there first and come back to get you."

"I like that you wanted to see me so badly you came to New York first."

"That's exactly how it was." He wanted to put a hand on her hip, run it down her thigh. He held back.

"You know, I don't mind the idea of fixing up an old house. It sounds kind of fun."

"Really? Or are you just trying to humor me?"

"No, really. The Hall certainly is beautiful. I just hope it's not too far gone to save."

"It shouldn't be that bad." Mason hoped that was true.

"Are there already cattle on the ranch?"

"No, we'll have to start from scratch."

"What about chickens?"

"Would you like chickens?"

"Well, don't get them just for me," she said. "I don't know if I'll stay. But I've always liked the idea of chickens."

"We'll definitely have chickens," Mason assured her, making a mental note to repair the coop as soon as possible. They'd always had chickens when he was growing up, but that was a long time ago. Still, baby chicks were just the sort of thing to warm a woman's heart. That and a well-mannered horse to ride.

REGAN WASN'T THINKING about chickens. She was thinking about Mason. Here in her bed. His chest was all she could have hoped it to be. Broad, muscled. And his abs… Definitely lickable. She touched them tentatively.

Mason's mouth quirked into a smile. "That's allowed."

"Is it?"

He covered her hand with his and brought it up to press her palm against his heart. She could feel it beating in his chest. Strong. Steady.

Like him. In the time they'd been together, she'd discovered that about him. He had a sense of humor. He was smart. But mostly he was rock solid—in his physique and in his personality.

He bent to kiss her and she melted against him, loving the press of his mouth on hers. When he gathered her into his arms she felt small and sexy. Her thin T-shirt barely shielded her from his touch. She wanted him to touch her all over.

"I like you, Regan Anderson. I like you a lot."

"I like you, too." She kissed him again.

A few minutes later they pulled away from each other and agreed it was time to get up. This was what torture felt like, Regan told herself as she showered. But when she was done and began to pack her bags, excitement overwhelmed her. She'd have nearly a month to spend with Mason and make up her mind about him. All those days.

And all those nights.

CHAPTER THIRTEEN

LATER THAT AFTERNOON, Mason fought back a wave of anticipation as he drove Regan from the airport through Chance Creek to swing by Great Aunt Heloise's assisted living facility on the northern edge of town. He'd rented a truck until he found one to buy, and as he drove he was gratified to see all the familiar landmarks of home. It hit him that this was all really happening. His military service was over and a whole new era of his life was opening up before him. He kept waiting for the depression his counselor had cautioned him about to kick in, but he didn't feel it. Not yet, anyway. All he felt was excited.

Regan eagerly looked out the window at the shops and restaurants they passed. "Are things the same as when you grew up here?" she asked.

"DelMonaco's is still there." He pointed to a family-style restaurant. "And there's the Dancing Boot." She frowned at the unlit neon sign and plain doorway. "It's a bar—it's better on the inside than the outside. There's Linda's Diner—great food at great prices."

"I don't see any Indian or Thai food," Regan said.

"How about sushi?"

"I doubt it, unless the place has really changed. But don't you fret; you'll find plenty that's good to eat around here."

Regan nodded, but she looked doubtful. Mason decided he'd take her to DelMonaco's as soon as possible. Maybe it wasn't a fancy New York restaurant, but he loved it. Or at least he had years ago.

"Hey—there's an Afghan food place! And Mexican! Both in one," Regan said excitedly, craning her head as they passed First Street. "I don't think I've ever seen that before."

Afghan food? That was new. Even Mexican was a stretch. Chance Creek had changed, after all.

They pulled into the parking lot of a sprawling complex. As far as assisted living facilities went, it was nice enough, the façade of the main building a combination of rough-hewn logs and glass windows. Inside was a reception area and a corridor that led to the common rooms. The individual apartments for seniors branched off in several directions. Mason led Regan to the reception desk.

"I'm here to pick up a key. My Great Aunt Heloise Hall said she'd leave it for me."

"I do have a note from Heloise." The receptionist shuffled through some papers. "Here it is. She's waiting for you in her room. One fifty one—it's just around that corner."

"She was supposed to just leave me the key."

The woman was apologetic but firm. "Sorry. All I

have is the note."

"It's no problem to say hi to your aunt. I bet she's excited to see you," Regan said.

Mason suddenly wished he'd left her in the car. What if Heloise blabbed about the deal she'd made with him and his brothers? "We'll only stop for a minute," he told Regan. Tension tightening his jaw, he followed the receptionist's directions to Heloise's apartment and knocked on the door. Heloise answered almost immediately and allowed Mason to give her a peck on the cheek.

"You've grown!" she announced as she ushered them to a small sitting room.

"An inch or two maybe, back in my teens." Mason grinned in spite of his worry. Heloise had shrunk at least that much. "We can't stay long, Heloise. We'll pick up the key and be on our way, then come back in a day or two for a real visit once we've gotten the lay of the land."

"Nonsense. You have plenty of time for a visit right now. Who's this?" She turned to Regan.

Mason sighed inwardly. This visit had the potential to be as dangerous as a sit down with an armed terrorist. "Heloise, meet Regan Anderson. Regan, this is my Great Aunt Heloise Hall."

"Nice to meet you," Regan said.

"Well, isn't she pretty?" Heloise said. She looked up at Mason. "Are you going to marry her?"

"I haven't proposed yet, if that's what you mean."

"You always were a slowpoke, Mason Hall. And

you've stayed away too long. That mother of yours ought to have brought you back before now."

"I know she's looking forward to coming back." He sat down next to Regan on a small couch, relieved that Heloise hadn't spilled the beans yet.

"When will she come?" Heloise poured them each a cup of tea and offered a plate of dry cookies. Regan took one and bit into it. Mason declined.

"Not until I build a house for her. That won't be until next year at the earliest."

"You bring her home as soon as you can. Family should be together. Speaking of which. When are your brothers arriving?"

"Austin will come in June, Zane by September. I'm not sure about Colt."

"Humph. I'll write him a letter. Set a fire under him."

Mason saw that Regan was smiling. "You want all your grand-nephews home, don't you?" she asked Heloise.

"Home, married and starting their families." She looked Regan up and down. "I hope you're not one of these women who think they'll be happier if they skip having children?"

"No, I'm planning on having a family."

"Humph. Good. Make him put a ring on your finger first."

"Heloise." Mason rolled his eyes. Same as ever.

"It's good advice." Heloise fixed him with a fierce look. "Men these days think nothing of getting women pregnant and running for the hills. They're like children themselves."

"I have no intention of knocking Regan up and heading for the hills." Damn it, he'd better rein in his tongue. If he riled the old girl up, who knew what she might say.

"No need to get vulgar."

Regan laughed, then bit her lip. "Sorry."

The corner of Heloise's mouth turned up. "I like you."

Regan grinned. "I like you, too."

Heloise turned back to Mason. "She'll do. Now take her home—the poor thing is exhausted and you're tramping her around like a circus train."

"Yes, Aunt Heloise." He stood up and offered Regan his hand. She took it and let him lead her to the door. "Regan, could you go on ahead and give me and my aunt a minute?"

"Of course. See you soon, Heloise." She slipped out into the hall and walked toward the entrance of the facility.

Mason turned to his aunt. "She doesn't know about your conditions for us keeping the ranch."

"I figured as much. I didn't give you away, did I? Tell me something, do you love that girl?"

Mason nodded. "I think I do. We're going to take some time to get to know each other better, though."

"Don't take too long. The clock's ticking."

"One other thing we haven't discussed. My brothers and I are going to put money in that ranch and if you change your mind at the end of the year, or if something happens and we can't fulfill your terms, we're going to be in a fix."

"You're asking if I intend to screw you over?"

"Now who's being vulgar?"

Heloise laughed. "Don't look so high and mighty. I was cussing long before you were a glimmer in your daddy's eye. To answer your question, no—I will not screw you over. If for any reason you fail at your attempt, I will pass the Hall on to Darren, but I will make you beneficiary to my own estate. It's not a lot, but it will be enough to reimburse you for your efforts, with a little left over. Unfortunately, you'll have to wait until I'm dead to get it."

"I'd prefer it if you stayed alive." He kissed her faded cheek.

"Me, too." She patted his arm. "You'll do fine, young man. You have your father in you. Now, get along with you."

Mason decided that was the best he could expect from Heloise. Ten minutes later, they were past the town's center heading south. The vista widened out again as ranchland spread to either side of the road. Far in the distance the Absaroka Mountains provided a beautiful backdrop for the spring-green pastures.

"It's lovely." Regan turned to him with a smile.

"This is home." How many times had he passed along this road as a child? He could picture his father's Ford F-250 like he was still riding in it. Mason's heart squeezed when for a second he felt the old man's presence beside him.

The finest piece of dirt you'll ever know. That's how Aaron had always described the ranch. Mason wished he was there to help them rebuild it. He wondered how it would feel to bring his mother back home to the property she'd loved so much. When he'd spoken to her, he'd told her not to get her hopes up yet—not until Heloise formally passed the land down to them—but he'd promised her he'd do everything he could.

"You boys and your wives won't want me in the Hall," she had laughed. "That's too many women already in one place."

"We'll build you a new home then."

"I'll take Zeke's old cabin," she said, but Mason shied away from that idea. He didn't like the thought of her in that sad place.

Fifteen minutes later they turned off the country road onto the dirt track that led to Crescent Hall. Already the proud house was visible on its rise of ground. Regan was quiet, taking in the tall gray structure with its wraparound porch, its corner tower and ornate details. With three above-ground stories, the Hall dominated the landscape. Mason knew there were barns and outbuildings beyond it, but these were hidden from the road on the downslope of the land.

"It's amazing." Regan leaned closer to the window, but Mason felt his jaw tighten. The closer they got to the Hall, the more evident the damage to the structure became. It appeared his uncle hadn't done a lick of work on the place in years. Shingles hung loosely on the roof, the paint on the porch railings and other details had almost all flaked away. He shuddered to think what might await them inside.

Regan grew quiet too as they approached, and by the time they pulled in before the house, Mason was tense with rage. While several broken windows had been covered with plywood, he counted at least three more that had been carelessly blocked with card-board—as if that would keep out the elements. The porch had sagged dangerously at the corner of the house. He could tell already most of it would need to be torn down and rebuilt—a large job he hadn't planned for.

"I didn't think it was this bad," he managed to say between clenched teeth to Regan before he got out of the car.

"It's nothing that can't be fixed." She joined him at the foot of the stairs to the porch.

"I hope you're right. Hold up—let me test these stairs and make sure they're safe." Mason tried them one at a time, pushing down on the emotions that swirled within his gut. He had to keep his temper on a leash, no matter what Zeke had done. He wasn't going to snap in front of Regan.

Not if he could help it.

Why hadn't Zeke called them when caring for it overwhelmed him? Why had he let it get so bad? Just to spite his nephews since he knew his own son wouldn't do what it took to run the ranch? What would his father think if he could see the Hall now?

He would just take in all the damage and make a plan to fix it. He wouldn't hang out here bellyaching—that was for sure. Aaron Hall was a doer, not a complainer. Mason resolved to follow his lead. He squared his shoulders and led the way up the stairs.

"This section of the porch seems strong enough. I don't know what happened over there." Most likely a support had rotted out. He moved to the front door and tried the knob. It was locked, but when he checked the mailbox he found the key. He hoped against hope the house hadn't been defiled inside by bored teenagers or petty criminals. When they entered the foyer, he was relieved to find it intact.

He tried the light switch beside the door and let out the breath he was holding when the electricity worked. A small, plain fixture in the center of the ceiling lit the room. Well, it wasn't as bad as it could have been. His anger ratcheted down a notch. He noticed Regan was frowning. "What is it?"

"I might as well admit I'm a renovation snob." She pointed at the light. "That's not even remotely accurate for the time period this house was built."

Mason shook his head. "It works, doesn't it?" She had no idea what a relief that was. If they'd had to re-wire the Hall, they'd be set back so far they'd never catch up again. As it was, his to-do list for getting the ranch in order was growing by leaps and bounds. He led the way into the room on the left, a formal dining room with wainscoting on the lower half of the walls. Nothing damaged in here, either, although the beautiful oak table and chairs they'd had when he was a child were gone. He swallowed against another surge of anger. Had Uncle Ezekiel sold all the furnishings? He hadn't budgeted for that, either.

Regan ran a hand over the white-painted wainscoting. She still looked troubled. He raised an eyebrow at her and she shrugged. "This paneling—look how thick the layers of paint on it are. It makes it look clumsy and I bet it was beautiful at one point."

Mason had never noticed the paint—it had always been like that, even in his childhood. Instead, he pictured his boisterous family crowded around the dining room table. When they roared with laughter, the old chandelier had shook and tinkled. The chandelier was gone—only dangling wires to show where it had been. "It's an old house, honey. Things have gotten painted a few times." He fought to keep his anger out of his voice. He wasn't mad at her, but he was furious with Zeke for vandalizing the home his family had loved. And worried about what else they would find. If Zeke hadn't cared for the house, what else hadn't he cared for?

"This is a beautiful house," she said fiercely. "Or it could be if anyone showed it any love."

Mason was taken aback by her vehemence, but before he could tell her that ranching didn't leave much time for interior decorating, she said, "It's just… I love old houses. Actually, I love all houses. They're a passion of mine. That's why when I got into finance, I ended up in loans. I love helping people qualify to buy their dream home. They always bring in the sales sheets they get from the realtor, and I get to see the photos and find out how many bedrooms and baths the house has, stuff like that. I have a whole folder of decorating ideas I've torn out of magazines over the years. The Hall is beautiful, Mason. It's exquisite. With the right care and renovations, it could be a show-stopper."

Mason softened. The Hall was already working its magic on her. Regan cared about the treatment it had received. She wanted to put it right. That meant she could picture herself living here, which meant she could see herself living with him. If she could look past its present state to see what it could be, that showed she was the kind of woman he'd hoped she was. He knew every nook and cranny—all the house's secrets. The knowledge that Regan could feel about it the way he did warmed his heart.

But what would they do for furniture? And what if Zeke had treated the barn, stables and other ranch buildings the same way he'd treated the Hall?

"Is that the kitchen?" Regan led the way through a connecting room into the big old-fashioned kitchen at the back of the house. More memories assailed Mason. An old woodstove dominated one of the back corners of the room. The other back corner had a door leading outside. There were the usual kitchen appliances, although these were hopelessly out of date.

This was where his father would dance with his mother as if no one else was looking. She loved to listen to music while she cooked the evening meal and even if she'd spent the day mucking about in the barns or with the cattle, she always took the time to spiff up for her husband before supper. He'd kiss her soundly on his way to the shower and by the time he came downstairs again he'd be fit to sit at her dining room table. Mason realized it was in these little gestures that his parents showed their love for each other.

Mason shook off the past and peered out the window, trying to assess the bunkhouse and barn from here. Neither building gave anything away at this distance, though.

"My grandmother had a refrigerator like this." Regan crossed to peer inside it. "I'm amazed this one still works."

"We might need to do some updating in here," Mason admitted. He had no idea how they were going to pay for that. Worry overtook him again.

"We don't have to update the refrigerator if it still works right. It's so retro. And I love this island." Regan moved to the large, rectangular butcher block island with cabinets underneath. "With a new stove this could be a wonderful kitchen. Oh, look at the view." She moved to stand beside him. Mason's mother had always complained that you couldn't see the mountains from this angle, but Regan was right; it was still pretty. He needed to get a good look at that barn, though, before he could appreciate details like that.

First things first; they'd finish touring the house. Another doorway led to a small hall with a tiny bathroom and laundry room off it, plus stairs down to the basement. Mason kept practicing his deep breathing as they passed by the shabby bathroom into the large living room. At one time this had been two rooms—a sitting room and a library—but his parents had combined the two to make a bigger space and Mason thought they'd done a good job. The room was spacious, yet comfortable, with a huge river rock fireplace topped with a thick wooden mantle. The back windows showed the view down to Chance Creek in the distance and the mountains far beyond.

"Now this is impressive." Regan spun in a circle to take it in.

It was, except for another broken window. Mason inspected the broken glass and the water stains on the hardwood floor in a semi-circle below it.

A quick tour through the rest of the house showed them wall-paper peeling in three of the four large bedrooms on the second floor, water damage in two more rooms with broken windows, and extensive damage to the tile floor in one of the second story bathrooms where his uncle had apparently replaced an older toilet with a new one, and struggled in the process. Regan had winced at that particular room and Mason couldn't blame her. The new toilet with its plastic seat and modern lines looked hideously out of place in the old-fashioned bathroom and his uncle hadn't even attempted to fix the floor.

Mason was too busy adding up the repair costs to care about the visuals, though. It was going to take money to make the house inhabitable by his brothers and their wives when they got married. Money they didn't have.

"How do you get to the third floor?" Regan asked when they'd seen all the bedrooms.

"Through here." He hoped Regan didn't notice the curtness of his voice as he indicated a narrow door at the end of the hall which when opened revealed a narrow set of steps. He led the way up them, hoping they wouldn't stumble on a colony of rats. It would be just his luck if they did.

To his relief, the third floor was warm and musty, but there was no evidence of leaks from the roof. Doors led off to small bedrooms where once servants would have slept, and a much larger room at the end of the hall that had once been the nursery. The carpets were old and threadbare and the rooms so narrow they couldn't house a queen sized bed, but Regan seemed interested in all the original details.

"I hadn't guessed you were so interested in interior design," he said distractedly when she pointed out the old-fashioned windows.

"Not so much interior design as the restoration of older properties. I used to go to open houses in the older sections of the city and pretend I was a prospective buyer, just so I could look at the places."

"Why didn't you buy anything?"

"In New York City? I'd be in New Jersey before I could afford anything."

"How come you didn't become an architect or something?"

She shrugged. "Finance seemed like a safer bet."

"Life isn't all about making safe choices." He moved close enough to take her hand, the truth of that staring him right in the face. How on earth would he pull off a renovation of the Hall on top of everything else they had to do to beat Heloise's deadlines? "Sometimes you have to make a leap of faith."

"I know," she said. "But sometimes you have to be a realist."

Was she trying to send him a message? He sure hoped not.

REGAN KNEW WHAT Mason was trying to tell her; that she should take a chance on him. Maybe she should. Maybe she would, but first she needed to know more about what she was getting into. The Hall was beautiful structurally, but in its present state it resembled something out of a gothic horror novel. It would take hard work and lots of it—not to mention money—to fix the place up the way it should look.

"We'll have to go through the place and take notes on what needs to be fixed." Mason held her hand when they started back down the narrow stairs, but his jaw was tight and she realized he hadn't been prepared for what they'd seen. "We'll need to estimate costs and prioritize the jobs. Purchasing cattle, horses and equipment take top priority. Without them, there's no use fixing the house because we won't have an income."

"Do you have a budget worked out?"

"I have a ballpark idea of what we'll need. Austin and Zane have told me what they can contribute. Colt has been a bit cagey."

"Why is that?" She followed him back downstairs to the front porch.

"He wants to stay in the military. He's not interested in coming home yet."

"Is that a problem?" She leaned against a post and crossed her arms over her chest. The sunshine felt good on her face.

"It could be," Mason admitted. "We could really use him."

"How much money do you have budgeted to fix the house?"

"Not enough," he said. "We'll have to do it in stages. Tackle the roof and kitchen first, I'd say. Replace all the broken windows. Then take it step by step as we have the money." He turned to her. "I'm sorry. The state of the house is probably rougher than you were expecting."

"It's a challenge," she said. "I like challenges."

"Do you?" His shoulders relaxed a fraction of an inch and he tipped her chin to bring her mouth to his. His kiss was thorough and melted her insides until she had to put a hand on his chest to steady herself. "I should have played harder to get, huh?"

"Probably." She chuckled. "I never expected to be here with you, you know."

"I expected it. Right from the start." His satisfied

smile made her tingle all over. This handsome, strong warrior had set his sights on her and she loved being the object of his attention. Loved knowing how much he wanted her. Loved knowing he'd done whatever it took to get her here.

"You're amazing." She reached up on tiptoes to give him a kiss. "Show me around outside."

"You've got it." He led her down the steps and around to the back of the house, where they crossed the yard to a long low building he called the bunk-house. Mason's footsteps slowed as they approached the building and Regan could see why. More windows were broken and the door opened to his touch. Inside, the rooms were dark and bare.

"Son of a bitch." He glanced her way. "Sorry, Regan—Uncle Zeke stripped the whole damn place here, too." Mason waved at the empty cupboards and counters in a room that should have been a kitchen. There was no refrigerator or stove, but there were spaces where they ought to be. He led the way to the opposite end of the building where a large room stood empty. "He sold the bunks, too. They were cast iron—original to the ranch."

Picking up his pace, he led the way back outside and over to a large barn. It too stood empty, with boards missing from its walls and a hayloft with a definite sway to it.

"Damn him to hell." Mason was off again, out the door and striding in the opposite direction of the house. Regan followed at a jog, her stomach in knots.

When Mason stopped abruptly and threw his hands up in the air, she knew he'd found another disaster.

"What is it?" she asked softly.

He gestured at the field ahead of him. At the corners and long intervals stood wooden posts. In between them metal uprights were evenly spaced. Some were vertical. Others were angled and some had been knocked down altogether.

She shook her head. "What's it for?"

He rounded on her. "It's a pasture. Or it would be, if it had a fence around it. He stole the goddamned wire! Or someone else stole it. Must have sold it for scrap." Mason's hands were balled into fists, his frustration plain to see. "It will take weeks to fix all this. We haven't even seen the stables yet." He took off again. Regan followed him more slowly this time, the truth dawning on her. The state of the ranch was far worse than Mason had imagined. Maybe he and his brothers didn't have the money it would take to fix it. What would happen then?

When she caught up with him again he was pacing the length of a small outbuilding. Its purpose wasn't apparent at first.

"All the tools are gone. All of them. Do you have any idea—" He cut off when he saw her face. Dropped his hands. "I'm sorry. None of this is your fault. Damn it, I should have never brought you here." He rubbed a hand over his buzz cut hair and she had the feeling he'd start to pull it out in another minute.

"Of course you should have. If we're going to

make a life together we have to be able to face trouble together."

"But I didn't mean for you to see it like this. I want you to love it here as much as I do."

She'd grown accustomed to Mason's face, but now it was all hard angles. He was furious at what he'd found here. He was trying to hide it, but he wasn't succeeding.

"I do love it. I mean—" What did she mean? Just a week ago she would have said she was a city girl. She still wasn't sure about ranching, but the Hall—it was a dream come true. "It's beautiful here and I haven't made my mind up yet, but I haven't seen anything to dissuade me from staying, either. I'll help you figure it out, whether I stay or go. I mean that."

His gaze searched her face. He nodded. "It's just—I have a timeline. And now—"

"A timeline?"

He sagged back against what she now saw was a workbench. "I should have told you before. Inheriting the ranch is based on some contingencies. My brothers and I have to get the cattle operation up and running before a year is up. Heloise doesn't expect us to turn a profit—it takes time to raise cattle—but we have to be able to carry a hundred pairs within twelve months. That means we need barns, pastures, stables for the horses, equipment to get in crops to feed to the animals over the winter. I thought we'd have all that."

"But you don't."

"We don't."

"Is there any way you can still pull it off?"

He took a breath. Looked her in the eye. "I don't know."

She'd never seen Mason anything other than fully confident and the change was startling. She had begun to think of him as super-human; some kind of real life James Bond. He didn't look defeated, though. Far from it. She could tell he was already adjusting his plans and coming up with new ones. Still, she could tell the state of the ranch was a blow.

"Show me something else," she said. "Something good. Something you loved about the place as a kid."

"Okay." Mason thought about it. "I'll show you two things." He took her on a ten minute walk down a track between two pastures until they reached a smooth flowing stream. "This is Chance Creek. It flows from the northeast through town and then south until it gets here. It turns southwest eventually." They stood on its banks admiring its clear water. Mason was regaining his equilibrium and now he drew her close. "This has always been one of my favorite places. In a month or so we'll be able to swim. My whole family used to come down here on sunny days for a break—even my mom and dad."

She smiled. He wasn't conceding defeat. "Can't wait." It occurred to her that she too wanted the plan to work. She would help Mason figure out how to get everything done. At least for the next few weeks—until she made her final decision.

They watched the water flow past and she could tell

his mind had drifted back to all of the ranch's problems. She wished she could offer him some advice, but she didn't feel qualified to give him any.

"The ranch is in worse shape than I expected," he echoed her thoughts, "but we're not beaten yet. I've been gone for a long time, but the Hall name still means something around here. I'll look up our neighbors and old friends and ask for a hand setting things to right. It'll still cost a pretty penny, but more hands will get the work done faster." He turned to her. "Just you wait and see—it'll be all right."

She believed him. Mason seemed capable of any miracle.

He tugged her hand. "Come on, let me show you something else." He led her back up the track and across the yard with a lighter step. They cut behind the Hall toward the woods. Mostly pine, but interspersed with hemlock and birch, it was a comfortable, mature forest—fairly clear of brush and undergrowth.

Regan cocked her head when she spotted a kind of wooden ladder ahead, then raised her brows in surprise when she realized it was more like a piece of playground equipment. Two identical pieces of playground equipment side by side, actually. "What is that?"

"That is the Course, as we like to call it. It's a side-by-side obstacle course. My dad got the idea when we were pretty young, after watching a show on television. He decided it would be the perfect thing to occupy four boys who had the tendency to get in fights and then expect him to sort them out. He built all the obstacles by hand, practiced on them for a while himself until he could run through it in a fraction of the time we could, and then relied on it for the next ten years."

"Relied on it how?"

"If we had a dispute, we ran the Course to see who won. If one of us had a complaint against him, we ran the Course against him. It goes without saying he always won. If we misbehaved, we had to run the Course and beat a certain time before we got our privileges back. Dad called it his one-size-fits-all-boy-sorting-out machine."

Regan frowned. "I'm not sure that's how parenting is supposed to work."

"Worked pretty well, actually. I'm sure a psychologist could have a field day with the whole thing, but it served two purposes. It stopped us from fighting, or at least gave us a way to sort out our fights. It got to the point where we took our grievances to the Course without Dad even having to tell us. It also made us strong. We all sailed through boot camp."

Regan remembered the feel of his muscles. She could believe it. "What did your mother say about it?"

Mason laughed. "She ran it a few times herself. My parents didn't fight often—they were more in love than any couple I've ever seen—but I remember one time they had a doozy of an argument over Uncle Zeke. Zeke had borrowed money from Dad and refused to pay it back. Mom thought they should demand to be paid. Dad thought they should let it slide. They got into a shouting match—just about the only time I heard them do that. It freaked Colt out something fierce. He was only about nine at the time. He told them if they were going to argue they'd better run the Course to find the winner." Mason's smile grew. "They did, too. They were like that—able to see the humor in things even when times were tough. By the time they were half-way through they were laughing fit to be tied. By the time they were done they'd forgotten all about that argument." He scratched the back of his neck. "They told us to go visit our cousin Darren for a few hours and headed back to the house to be alone."

Regan grinned. She liked the picture that story painted of his childhood. No wonder the loss of his father and the Hall had been so devastating to his whole family. "Let's see it."

"See what?"

"The Course. Let's see you run it."

"What? Now?"

"Unless you're chicken." Regan bit her lip to keep from smiling. As if Mason was ever chicken. But maybe it would distract him from his worry about the ranch for a little longer.

"Those are fighting words, woman." He stepped away from her and stripped off his shirt. Regan whistled. "You need to see my muscles to get the full effect," he said, grinning.

"No complaints here."

Mason positioned himself near one of the sets of monkey bars. Just like the ones at her elementary school, they looked like two vertical ladders holding up a horizontal one. The horizontal one had rungs all the way across, while the vertical ones just had a few at the bottom to give a boost to kids too small to gain access to the top ones.

"You need to call my start."

"Okay. On your mark. Get set. Go!"

Mason exploded off the starting line, leaped for the horizontal rungs of the monkey bars and went hand over hand across them in a flash, skipping two rungs at a time. He was right—the play of his muscles was something to behold, but before she could enjoy it too much he was off the bars and running—sprinting—to the next obstacle. Regan spotted a straight path that seemed to run through the center of the Course. She dashed down it to keep Mason in sight as he raced for a vertical wooden wall that looked to her like it was ten feet tall.

Maybe not quite that tall, she thought when Mason hurled himself at it, gripped the top with his fingertips, pulled a leg up and over and dropped out of sight behind it. Regan, stunned by that spectacle, nearly forgot to dash forward to see what was next. When she caught up again, he was racing through a bunch of old tires laid out horizontally on the ground, like a football player doing drills. His feet moved so fast she was sure he'd trip, but she reminded herself he'd done this hundreds of times. Maybe thousands.

Mason kept his footing, sprinted forward fifty feet and threw himself to the ground to army-crawl under low lines of what she realized was real barbed wire. Shocked that anyone would let boys play near something so dangerous, she lost track of Mason again when he sprang back up to his feet and raced away.

By the time she caught up he'd passed through several obstacles and was approaching what looked like an enormous balance beam made from a tree trunk. The beam itself was about thirty feet long. The trunk of the tree that had been felled to make it was roughly a foot and a half in diameter. What made the obstacle truly frightening was its height. A good ten feet in the air, Regan estimated. Thick logs sloped upward on either end from the ground to offer access on and off the giant beam. There were no handholds that she could see on them. Just plain logs, polished over time by the hands and feet of the Hall boys.

Mason approached the closest incline at full speed and to Regan's amazement he dashed straight up it. Reaching the top, he didn't stop to get his balance, although his pace finally slowed. He walked across the log quickly, keeping his eyes focused ahead. Regan watched, her heart in her mouth, not breathing again until he skidded down the far incline and reached solid ground again.

He wasn't just a SEAL. He was an athlete, she realized. His body was beautiful. Powerful.

Breathtaking.

She watched him complete the rest of the obstacles including one she'd seen on television but never seen in real life—a salmon ladder. Thick, vertical metal uprights had been attached to each of two pine trees growing close together. The uprights had heavy prongs that stuck out of them at even intervals in forty-five degree angles. A metal chin-up bar rested in the lowest set of these prongs. Mason gripped it, swung his legs hard and popped the bar up into the next higher set of prongs. He did this again and again, climbing up the ladder by popping the bar into ever-higher sets. His muscles bunched and worked. Regan was mesmerized. She'd always thought that particular stunt was fake.

When she realized Mason was nearly done with the obstacles, she dashed back to the starting point, which was also where the course ended. Soon after, Mason reached the finish line, out of breath, sweating, but not done in. Instead, she would swear the course had invigorated him. She felt puny and out of shape next to this amazing specimen of human capability.

"That was incredible," she admitted when he'd caught his breath.

"You liked it, huh?"

"I have no words." She touched his arm, felt the muscles at play beneath his skin. "I couldn't do half those things."

"You could if you had as much practice as I've had." He picked up his shirt and used it to wipe himself down. "Did it turn you on?" He came to her. Hitched his thumbs through her belt loops. Tugged her closer.

"It did," Regan was forced to admit. "A lot." In fact, it set her on fire. She was aware of Mason in a whole new way now. Aware of his strength. His capabilities. Aware of every muscle in his back, shoulders, abs and arms. No wonder he'd made such a career for himself in the military. He must have stood head and shoulders over the other men in terms of physical fitness. She knew him well enough by now to guess that he stood head and shoulders above them in intelligence, as well. Mason was a hell of a man.

"Good. Mission accomplished." He bent down to kiss her. This kiss was different than the ones that had gone before and Regan wondered if that was because they were on Mason's turf now.

Home field advantage, she thought dizzily as his kiss deepened and her body responded. He was right; she was turned on. Her hands explored his shoulders, back, and biceps of their own volition, wanting to feel the muscles she'd watched at play. Her mouth answered his, kissing him with an intensity she couldn't dial back. She found herself pressed against him but still unsatisfied, and when his embrace tightened she moaned in frustration. It still wasn't enough.

When Mason's hands tugged lightly at the hem of her t-shirt, Regan answered his unspoken question quickly. She was ready to take this next step with him—more than ready. Maybe she should wait. Maybe she should take this slow and easy, one step at a time, but she'd never felt this hunger for a man before and she wanted Mason's hands on her skin. She yanked her shirt up and over her head, barely pulling away from him to accomplish the maneuver. As soon as it was gone, she lurched forward and kissed him again, already fumbling at the catch of her bra. She wanted it off. Wanted it gone.

Mason chuckled against her. "Let me help you with that."

She felt small, delicate, womanly as his large hands covered hers and released the catch. She yanked the bra off and tossed it away. Seized his wrists and lifted his hands to cup her breasts. Her breath hitched almost in a sob when he did so, sliding his palms over her pliant skin. Squeezing.

When his thumbs traced over her nipples, Regan arched back and Mason bent down and kissed one rosy peak, then the other. Regan thrust her breasts forward to allow him greater access and was rewarded when he took one nipple into his mouth. He suckled it until she was weak in the knees, clinging to him to stay upright.

She hardly noticed when he lowered her to the ground, spreading her shirt beneath her. Dried leaves on the forest floor itched crisp and dry beneath her shoulders. Above her, Mason stripped quickly, unbuckling his pants and kicking them off. He dropped his shorts and knelt above her, giving her all the time in the world for a good, long look.

When he finally lowered himself on top of her, Regan could hardly breathe for wanting him. He waited while she undid her own jeans, slid them down and shimmied out of her panties as well. Pinned by his gaze, turned on by it more than she could express, she waited for him.

She wasn't disappointed.

"Are you sure about this?" Mason said, lying down beside her and taking her into his arms. "I don't want to ruin things between us. Don't feel you have to."

"I want to. More than anything."

His features softened at her admission. "You know I'd do anything for you. I want to make all of this shine again." He gestured to the ranch. "Just for you. You've given me a reason to bring it back to life again."

"I can't wait to see it when you're done."

He traced a hand down her shoulder. Ran a finger over the swell of her breast. She shivered with anticipation, and he moved closer. "I wish you could see it now. I wish it wasn't in such bad shape. If I'd known, I'd never—"

"Shhh." She put a finger to his lips. "We'll build it back up together and it will be even more special."

His arms tightened around her. "How'd I get lucky enough to find you?"

"I found you, remember?"

He kissed her again, positioning himself between her legs. "I want to make love to you, Regan."

She nodded her assent. He fished a condom out of his jeans and slid it on. For a long moment he hesitated, his gaze holding hers, requiring her full attention, waiting for her to grant him access.

"Hurry," she said finally, the word half-whisper, half-entreaty.

Mason bent down to kiss her, surrounding her with his arms. He gathered her close and entered her in one, hard thrust.

Regan gasped, then moaned as he pulled out and thrust in again. He filled her so completely, set every nerve in her body alight. The weight of him above her turned her on even more. She raked her fingers over his ass, relishing the play of his muscles, and urged him on.

MASON NEEDED LITTLE urging. He couldn't hold back if he wanted to—not when he'd waited this long to be inside Regan. She was hot, ready, and more than willing. She'd torn off her clothes like she couldn't wait and he blessed her for it, since that saved him the trouble of feeling like a heel for tearing them off of her. All thoughts of taking it slow and easy had gone straight out of his mind the moment he laid her down on the ground. He knew their first time should have been somewhere better than this. He should have brought a blanket, at least.

Too late. The ground would have to do. Tangled up with her, lost in the feel of her, all he could do was thrust again and again, press kisses to her mouth and throat, wrap his arms around her and hope she understood. He was crushing her, her breasts flat against his chest, his hands wrapped in her hair, but she didn't struggle against him. She was as on fire for him as he was for her. The only mistake he could make was to stop.

Mason didn't stop. He kicked things up a notch, lowering his hands to her ass, lifting it to get even deeper access. Regan cried out as he thrust himself home, her body moving with his. Mason moved faster, deeper and she met him stroke for stroke. Just when he didn't think he could hold on much longer she cried out and shuddered in his arms in her release. Mason followed her quickly, grunting as he plunged into her again and again. When he finally collapsed on top of her, he was more out of breath than he'd been at the end of the Course. Beneath him Regan chuckled.

"You know how to give a girl a workout."

He stiffened. "I didn't hurt you…"

She shushed him with a kiss. "You didn't hurt me, Mason Hall. And don't you dare take it slow and easy with me. Fast and hard is just the way I like it."

"Good." Mason's voice rumbled in his throat. "Because that's just the way I like it, too." He rolled off of her and pulled her with him. "And as soon as I make you my wife we'll do that without the condom." His mouth quirked into a smile. "What do you think about that?"

REGAN WELCOMED MASON'S arm around her waist as they walked back toward the Hall. She felt dizzy, nearly overcome by the force of their lovemaking and the intensity of her release. She was no shy virgin, but making love to Mason was something entirely different than she'd known before. Was it because of the circumstances or because of the man, she wondered. Either way, it could be addictive. She already knew she wanted to be with him again.

Then there was his question. What did she think about them making a child together? When they got married.

Not if. When.

The thought made her hot.

A child with Mason. A child with this man who was turning out to be everything she'd ever wanted. She kept thinking that she'd blink and find herself out of this fairy-tale and back into everyday life.

So she chuckled when they re-entered the house and climbed the stairs to the dilapidated second story bathroom. How much more real could life get? The tiles were cracked or missing. The sink was caked with dirt. There was no shower curtain, but Mason fetched a scrub brush and a can of powdered cleanser and attacked the claw-foot tub until it was spotless while Regan watched, once more astonishing her.

"Learned that in the military," he said briefly when she raised an eyebrow. "Impressed?"

"Extremely." She'd never watched a man clean a tub before.

He drew a bath and they both climbed in, taking up positions at opposite ends. The hot water made Regan feel boneless and she lay back against the curved sides of the tub, watching Mason watch her back.

"Like what you see?" he finally asked, tugging on her ankle.

"I do. A lot."

"Good. I like what I see, too." He caressed her

foot, massaging her instep, and Regan closed her eyes. She luxuriated in the hot water and the feel of his fingers squeezing and kneading first one foot and then the other. Even his fingers were strong, she thought, as well-being spread through her. "Don't fall asleep," Mason cautioned her with another tug.

"I'm going to, if nothing exciting happens," she murmured. She opened her eyes when Mason found her hand and tugged her forward. She grumbled, but allowed him to pull her until she floated above him. He turned her over and tugged her down until she lay atop him, her seat pressed into his lap.

He was hard again. Noticeably so. As Regan wriggled against him, she came fully awake. Mason drew her down until she lay back against his chest, then soaped up his hands and ran them over the length of her body. The combination of the hot water, Mason's muscled form beneath her and his slick hands running up and down over her skin set Regan on a slow burn all over again. He caressed her breasts, squeezing and kneading and teasing her nipples into hard peaks. In turn, Regan shifted against his hardness, until the hitch in his breath told her he wanted more.

She wanted more, too. They played until both of them could hardly hold back, then there was an awkward moment while Mason sheathed himself, both of them needing to get to their knees in the tub for him to be able to perform the maneuver, after grabbing yet another condom from the jeans he'd ditched on the bathroom floor. Regan thought about teasing him for his forethought, but suddenly Mason was beneath her again, his hardness prodding her. Opening her. And she was far too thankful to tease him.

This new position made for a whole new series of sensations and soon Regan was arched back against Mason's chest as his hands molded and kneaded her breasts and his thrusts set her body alight. When he gripped her hips and pulled her down against him, he entered her so fully she shattered with an intensity that had her crying out his name. Mason came with her, his movements pushing her to higher heights and when their passion ran its course, Regan could hardly breathe for wanting him more.

Mason circled his arms around her, and she knew what he wanted to say. That she had to stay with him. That he wouldn't let her go. That was fine with her, she thought as her heart rate slowed.

She never wanted to leave.

WHEN IT WAS time for dinner, Mason drove Regan back into town to DelMonaco's. They stopped at a store on the way and picked up pads of lined paper and pens in order to come up with a new plan of attack, as Mason called it. He brought along the timeline he'd already constructed to use as a guide, but told her what they'd found at the ranch had made it obsolete.

"Think of this as your last supper," he told her after the hostess led them to their table and took their drink order. "Because from here on in it's going to be work, work and more work." He looked away as the truth of that statement hit him.

"What's wrong?"

"I meant to bring you to the ranch and sweep you off your feet. But now—" He shrugged. Maybe he'd bitten off more than he could chew. It would take all his time and attention to have a shot at fixing everything Zeke had broken, even with help from friends and neighbors. What would he have left over to give to Regan?

"You already swept me off my feet." She must have kicked her shoes off under the table because her toes were caressing his shin through his jeans. Mason smiled in spite of the seriousness of the situation they found themselves in. "We'll do it together. What better way to get to know each other than by going through a crisis together, right?"

His heart warmed at the way her eyes shone. He knew exactly how she felt. As grave as things were at the ranch, her presence here made it hard to feel fear. Surely there wasn't anything he couldn't do with her looking on. Still, Regan had never been on a ranch before—she didn't know what they faced.

What would his father have done in a similar situation? Would he have shipped his mother off to her relatives while he got to work?

His lips quirked at the thought of that scenario. His mother would have given him hell if he'd tried such a thing. She was small and slight, but she was a firecracker, too. She could work like a demon and still laugh and tease her husband enough to make him drop his tools and tackle her. She would never consent to be sent away when times got tough.

What about Regan, though?

"What do we do first?" She waited for his answer, interest dancing in her hazel eyes. Her auburn hair curled around her pretty face and fell in waves over her shoulders. He wanted to run his fingers through it, pull her close and kiss her again. Her enthusiasm made his heart lift. He wouldn't send her away. As long as she wanted to be part of the renovation, he'd welcome her with open arms. He just hoped she knew what she was getting into.

Together, they constructed lists of the chores they'd need to accomplish before they brought cattle and horses to the ranch, and Mason was pleasantly surprised by Regan's quick understanding and helpful suggestions. She may not know ranching, but she had common sense, and that counted for a lot. As they worked he found his thoughts growing graver again, though. The task ahead of them was just about impossible to achieve in the short time they had. He wasn't a quitter any more than his father had been, but this was more than an uphill climb—it would be like scaling a cliff.

"Mason Hall? Is that you?"

Mason looked up to see their waitress at the end of the table. She was young and blond with her hair pulled back into a high pony-tail.

"Sarah-Jane?" Mason blinked. "Well, I'll be…"

"I'm surprised you recognize me," she said with a laugh. "I was only ten or eleven when you left town." She turned to Regan. "I don't think we've met before, though." She extended a hand.

Regan shook it. "I'm Regan Anderson. This is my first time in Chance Creek."

"You'll love it here," Sarah-Jane said confidently. She turned back to Mason. "Are your brothers back?"

"Not yet, but they will be. We're the advance guard—just arrived today. We plan to fix up the Hall so it's ready for them to come home to."

"Sounds great. Let me know if I can be any help." Sarah-Jane took their orders and then paused, her expression turning serious. After a moment, she said, "You know, I hate to be the one to tell you this, but maybe I should give you a head's up. If you just got here, no one else might have said anything yet. I'd hate for you to hear about it from someone who's angry." She bit her lip, still holding her order pad and pen in her hand. "You know Zeke was having money trouble when he passed, don't you? I mean, I heard the Hall had gotten pretty rough."

"Yeah." He wasn't sure where this was headed, but he didn't like the sound of it. Sarah-Jane obviously had some bad news to impart.

"He left some debts." She made a face. "He left a lot of debts, actually. If you've taken over the Hall, people might expect you to make them good. I don't think that's fair," she rushed on to say, "but it's the way things are."

Debts? Mason's heart sank. "Do you know who he owed?"

"He had a tab down at Rafters, I know that for sure. Heather told me."

"Heather Ward? She's still in town?" That name was a blast from the past.

"Yep—she's right over there, actually. I imagine the others will make themselves known. Sorry to be the bearer of bad news."

"That's all right. I'm glad you told me." But he wasn't glad to find out that Zeke had thrown another stumbling block in his path. Now he was responsible for his uncle's bar tab? What about Darren? Why didn't everyone Zeke owed knock on his door instead?

Mason knew the answer to that. For one thing, Darren lived over near Bozeman now, and by all accounts he was barely scraping by. If Zeke had run the Hall into the ground, he probably didn't have much money to leave to his son when he passed away. Plus Darren had a passel of kids who still lived at home. And he wasn't the one who had inherited the Hall. It was family tradition to pass the ranch down as a single parcel from generation to generation, which is why Mason's father had co-owned it with Zeke, and why Mason would co-own it with his brothers. As long as any of them was alive, the ranch would remain in the hands of this generation. Only when all four of them had died would it pass on.

No, it was Mason that people would come to. He shook his head. He was beginning to think he'd stumbled into quicksand when he'd come back home. He searched the restaurant until he spotted Heather seated at a table with another woman and a man. She had dark, curly hair, and wore a yellow shirt and jeans that looked poured on. She was still as slim as she'd been in high-school. Just as curvy, too. She'd been one of the prettiest girls in his school, and she and Austin had hardly left each other's side until their messy breakup just before his father had died. Mason hadn't thought about her in years.

"What are the chances you'd know our waitress?" Regan said when Tracey left.

"Around here? Pretty good." He was still looking at Heather, though. He could picture her and Austin walking arm and arm through the halls of Chance Creek High. It made him feel old.

"Heather certainly is pretty."

Mason's attention snapped back to Regan. He didn't want her to get the wrong idea. "She's Austin's old girlfriend. They dated in high school. Broke up just a few weeks before my father died.

"Are you sure she's *Austin's* old girlfriend?" Regan asked lightly when he glanced her way again.

"What? Yeah, I'm sure." He was glad when Sarah-Jane arrived with their salads and rolls. Anything to break the sudden tension. He supposed he should be grateful Regan cared enough about him to feel jealous, but he was wary of anything that could change her mind about sticking around long enough to fall in love with him.

"Are we going to sleep at the Hall tonight?" Regan asked him.

"I planned on it, if that's okay with you. Now, if there was hay in that hayloft, I'd show you a real good time." Or he would if the hayloft didn't have a sag to it that had him worried.

"I didn't notice any furniture."

She was right. Uncle Zeke had stripped the place bare. Most of the curtains were gone along with the beds, dressers, desks and other furniture. He reached across and took her hand. "Do you mind roughing it for one night? Tomorrow we'll buy a decent bed."

She looked at him. "One bed?"

"After this afternoon I think we can share a bed." He grinned. "Don't you?"

"I suppose. As long as we can grab that tower room." She ducked her head.

He liked the way a blush pinked her cheeks. If they weren't in a public place, he'd lean over and—

"Mason?"

He dropped Regan's hand and faced Heather Ward, who stood at the end of their table, her face slack with shock.

"Heather…"

"What are you doing here?"

"I've come home to fix up the Hall and get the ranch on its feet again. Good to see you."

Her glance fell on Regan and he hurried to introduce them. "Regan, meet Heather Ward. Heather, meet Regan. My… girlfriend."

Regan's gaze snapped to him and she smiled. He smiled back. She hadn't denied it.

"Are the rest of your brothers here?"

He noticed her attempt at nonchalance and matched it, wondering if she still carried a torch for Austin after all these years. "No. Not now. Are you… okay?" Heather was looking paler by the minute.

"Fine, just fine. That's great. You've decided to come back home."

"Yep."

"Well, come by the store if you need any supplies. I work at Renfree's now."

"Renfree's Home Décor?"

"That's the one."

"Sarah-Jane said you worked at Rafters."

"You were asking about me?"

"Not exactly. She was telling me Zeke owed you money."

"Not me—Rafters. And Sarah-Jane's right on both counts. I work there too, and Zeke had racked up quite a tab when he passed away. You'll have to take that up with the owner."

"I'll do that."

She looked them over again and shook her head. "Well, it's nice to meet you, Regan. I hope you're happy here." She turned on her heel and strode from the restaurant.

"She seems… nice," Regan said uncertainly.

"I'm not sure nice is the word I'd use. Did she seem uneasy to you?"

Regan nodded.

He rubbed his chin. "She and Austin split up on bad terms. That was a pretty crazy time."

"Seems like a long time to hold a grudge about a high school breakup."

"My thought exactly. Well, they'll sort it out, I guess. Meanwhile, I'll have to sort out Zeke's debts before we can do anything else.

REGAN WOKE WHEN a beam of sunlight shone through the dirty bedroom window and nearly blinded her when she opened her eyes. She rolled onto her side and took in Mason's broad shoulders poking out from the sleeping bags they'd zipped together the night before. The day was already warm and the confines of the sleeping bags were downright steamy, but she hated to move and wake him. She wanted to prolong the glorious night they'd spent together in this fairy tale tower bedroom.

What were the chances she'd meet a man who could set her on fire again and again? Mason had been tense through dinner and while they shopped for the sleeping bags, and when they'd returned to the Hall he'd paced the rooms for a while. But later he'd calmed down as they sat on the back porch drinking beer and watching the sunset. It was cool, so Mason had tucked her in close to him and kept an arm around her. Slowly but surely his anger had dissipated until he could laugh again. They made out a little, and soon couldn't keep their hands off each other. When Mason led her upstairs to bed, her whole body had thrummed with anticipation. They'd stayed up for hours exploring each other's bodies, murmuring about their plans together, touching and stroking and teasing each other until they had to make love again.

The angle of the light told her it was still early. She did her best to slide out from the sleeping bags without waking him, but Mason's eyes snapped open the moment she moved. He smiled a slow, tender smile that left her weak in the knees.

"Hello."

"Hi." She felt shy suddenly, as if she hadn't given him access to every secret part of her the night before.

"You're even more beautiful in the morning."

Regan blushed. She knew her eyes must be shining with everything she felt for this man. She didn't mind; she wanted him to know her heart.

"I had a great time last night," he said.

"Me, too."

"I wish we could stay here all day, but there's lots to do."

"Including buying a real bed." She was sore from sleeping on the hard floor.

"Uh-huh."

"What about your brothers? Should we buy beds for them, too?"

Mason frowned and she wanted to smooth away the lines on his forehead. "Austin won't arrive until the middle of June. Zane will get here in the fall. And

Colt," he shrugged his shoulders. "Who knows about Colt? I hope to change his mind by next spring. We'll wait to buy their beds." The thought of replacing all the family heirlooms with impersonal store bought furniture depressed him.

"What's wrong?"

He shrugged. "Zeke sold all our stuff. It won't be the same with all new things."

"Were your furnishings antiques?"

"Not really. Just... old friends, I guess you could say."

"Do you have any pictures of the Hall from when you were young? Photos that might show the furniture?"

"My mom does. Why?"

"Have her send some over. We could hit estate sales and thrift stores. Auctions. I bet we could find some similar pieces."

It was a good idea. Except for the money. "Our furniture budget will be next to nothing."

To Mason's surprise, Regan smiled. "That's the challenge of it, then. Leave it to me. I'm the financial wizard, remember?"

"Okay." He bent down and kissed her. He'd gladly leave the furniture up to her. "I thought I'd have to work a lot harder to convince you to stay. It seems like the place is growing on you."

"It is," she admitted. "So are you."

"Oh, yeah? I hope you still feel that way tonight."

"Why, what are you going to do to me today?" She

wriggled her eyebrows. He could do just about anything he liked, as far as she was concerned.

"Put you to work. I want to test your small engine repair skills." He scooped her into his arms and blew a raspberry against her throat. Regan struggled to get away, laughing.

"I already told you I lied about that particular skill."

"Good thing you have some others." His hands slid to cup her ass. "Important ones." He rolled over onto his back and propped her up on top of him. "Hmmm. You feel good."

Regan bit her lip. She did feel good. So good. She had a feeling she knew where this was going, too.

But before she enjoyed another romp in the sack—literally—with Mason, it was time for her to come clean. She'd never expected to fall for him so hard, but she had and she couldn't keep secrets from him anymore. "I have to tell you something."

Mason stilled. "That sounds ominous."

"Not ominous, exactly. Just something you need to know."

"Okay."

"I'm having a baby."

Mason surged upright, nearly dumping her off his lap. He caught her with an arm around her waist. "You're pregnant?" His sharp gaze held hers.

"No—not yet. I mean—" She stared up at him helplessly.

"Explain." His tone made her quail. This was the warrior side of Mason. Hard. Unforgiving.

"I didn't think I'd find anyone," she blurted. "I decided to have a baby on my own. I've been through all the preliminary appointments. I picked this month to get pregnant. I'm due to ovulate just after the twenty-sixth. As soon as I do, I'm getting artificially inseminated."

Mason blinked "Artificially inseminated?"

"Like your cows." She spread her hands wide. "No bulls, just turkey-basters. You know."

His fingers tightened their grip. "So there's no man involved. No boyfriend? Fiancé?"

"No. I told you there hasn't been anyone in ages. I gave up."

"But then you met me." He leaned closer.

"But then I met you."

He scooped her up with a single arm, flipped her onto her back on the thin foam pad and straddled her, one hand curling around each of her biceps to hold her firmly in place. "Forget the turkey baster. I can do it so much better. Admit it." He dropped a kiss on her lips, which were parted in surprise. They twitched.

"How it gets done isn't the issue." She wriggled but he didn't loosen his hold. "It's what comes after."

"Would you rather be a single mother in the city or raise a family out here with me?"

"I have to choose right now?"

He growled. "You know the right answer."

She chuckled. "Maybe. But I'm not absolutely sure yet, and until I'm absolutely sure I'm not getting pregnant." She struggled to a sitting position and

Mason let her go. "You said you'd give me time to decide whether or not this is right for me. I'll give you my answer before the twentieth. Between now and then we can do a trial run."

"A trial run, huh?"

"That's right. We'll act like we're already married and see how we like it." She leaned forward and kissed him, her hand flat against his chest.

"Then let's get started, wife. We've got a long day ahead of us." He slid his hands down to cup her ass.

It was over an hour before they managed to get dressed.

Later that morning in Dundy's Hardware, she pushed a small metal shopping cart while Mason loaded it up with every tool imaginable. Some she recognized, but others she didn't. The scope of the work ahead of them began to take shape in her mind. Mason had shown her his revised timeline and although the extent of the repairs ahead of them were daunting, it energized her to know they were going to do it together. The more she thought about renovating the Hall, the more the idea intrigued her. She itched to go online and research the subject, but now was not the time. There was so much else to do first. As Mason picked out tool after tool, she thought about all the jobs on his timeline for the next few weeks. They'd have to work from morning until night to have any hope with keeping up with his lists. She wasn't sure it was humanly possible to finish them in time.

Mason kept her close as they shopped, as if his

body might convince her to partner with him since his words had failed. Regan had to admit it was working. The way he kissed her in out-of-the-way corners, held her hand as they walked down the aisles, and constantly found excuses to surround her with his arms as he pulled things off the shelves had her buzzing with longing for him again.

Right now, however, he was examining two reciprocating saws as if their lives depended on him choosing the right one. She waited patiently, taking the opportunity look him over once again. Mason Hall was as delicious as an ice cream sundae. No wonder she kept wanting more.

Mason glanced at her suddenly, smiled sheepishly, and set the two reciprocating saws back on their shelves. "I can get pretty focused. Sorry."

"Take your time. You don't need to treat me with kid gloves, Mason. We're in this together."

"I appreciate that." He tilted her chin up to kiss her. "I hope you realize how hard this is going to be. We won't have a moment to ourselves these next few weeks. I wanted to wine you and dine you and take you all over the ranch and town so that you'd never want to leave, but instead I'm going to work you to the bone. You'll probably pack your bags and move right back to that weenie apartment of yours."

"Weenie, huh? I'll have you know that's large by New York standards."

"Good thing you found yourself a Montana man, then." He pulled her into an embrace and slipped his hands under the waistband of her jeans.

"No one could call you weenie," she agreed and leaned into his kiss. A white-haired woman in a Dundy's Hardware smock rounded the corner of the aisle, took them in and retreated again. Regan pulled away, giggling. "We're making a spectacle of ourselves."

"Who cares?" But he let her go, grabbed one of the saws and put it into the basket with a confidence that had been slipping moments before. Regan promised herself that she'd do whatever it took to make those deadlines.

When they reached the till, they found themselves in line behind a pretty, curvy blonde in a sundress and cowboy boots, a tiny shrug sweater her only concession to the fact that the weather, while pleasant, wasn't hot.

"Emma? Emma Larson?"

"Mason Hall! I heard you were back in town."

News must travel fast around here, Regan thought as the two hugged. Mason turned to her. "This is Emma Larson. She took riding lessons at the ranch when she was a kid."

"You were a kid yourself." Emma grinned up at him. "You liked to think you were hot shit, though."

"I've always been hot shit."

Regan laughed along with them, despite the twinge of jealousy she felt. Everyone in town seemed to know and like Mason. It made her feel like an outsider.

"I thought I heard you'd moved away," Mason said. They advanced in line, the young woman working the till starting to check through Emma's purchases.

"I did." Emma shrugged. "I just got back a week ago. I'm staying with my grandmother for the time being, but I have my eye on a shop in town with an apartment over it. I've got an appointment next week with a loan agent."

Regan perked up. "Do you have all your information gathered?"

"I hope so. This is all new to me; I've never bought property before."

"I could look through what you have and make a few suggestions," Regan offered. "I mean," she glanced at Mason. "If you want me to. You don't even know me." She felt her cheeks heat.

"Do you know about loans?" Emma cocked her head.

"That's my job. Or—it was my job. Back in New York City. I was a loan officer at a bank there."

"Wow! I'd love to have you look my paperwork over. Could I take you to lunch tomorrow?"

Regan thought about the timelines Mason had placed on the kitchen table and shook her head. "I can meet you for coffee after dinner tomorrow night. How about eight o'clock. Is that too late?"

"That's terrific! Linda's Diner okay?"

"Sure."

Emma paid for her purchases and left with a wave. Regan turned to Mason. "You don't mind me helping Emma, do you?"

"As long as you don't leave me alone for too long."

"Mr. Hall, do you mind waiting a minute? I need to

get my supervisor." The cashier's voice broke into their conversation. She looked them over with frank curiosity. Her name tag read Susan.

Mason looked thoughtful. "Do I know you? I can't place your face."

She shook her head. "No, we've never met before. I just heard Emma say your name and put two and two together. Mr. Dundy told us that if you came in we needed to get him. He wants to talk to you."

Regan waited silently beside Mason while Susan went off to fetch the owner. She came back with a dour man in his late sixties, who shook Mason's hand.

"Sorry about your loss, son."

"Thank you. Good to see you, Albert." Mason's voice was friendly, but cautious. Regan thought she knew what he was worried about. Albert Dundy looked like he wanted to dispense with the civilities as soon as possible and move right along to the business at hand. She could only imagine what that business was.

"I have a matter to discuss with you. Do you want to come into my office?"

Mason glanced around. There were no other customers nearby. "Right here will do fine. Let me guess—Zeke owed you money."

"That's right." Albert folded his arms across his chest. "A lot of money, and I figure you're the one to see to set it right."

A muscle ticked in Mason's cheek. Regan was angry on his behalf. She knew he meant to make good on all Zeke's debts, so why was Albert acting like he was trying to get away with something?

"How much?"

"About forty-five hundred."

Mason didn't move, but she could tell the number was a blow.

"I'll take care of that in a couple of days when I set up a checking account in town."

"And I'll sell you those tools when you do." Albert indicated all the supplies they had loaded onto the checkout counter.

"You're kidding, right? I'm good for it, Albert—it would just be easier when I've moved my cash."

"Zeke made lots of excuses and promises, too. I've already lost enough money to the Halls. I'm not losing any more."

The more Albert talked, the more Susan seemed to shrink into herself behind the counter. It was obvious the woman would have liked to be anywhere but here.

Mason looked like he was about to lose his temper, but he kept his voice calm. I can use a credit card or I can write you an out-of-state check. Which would you prefer?"

"Credit card." Albert motioned Susan aside as Mason fished his wallet out of his pocket. He rang up the tools and added the extra amount to the bill. Mason went through the steps to use his credit card silently, but Regan was sure he was fuming inside. She had a feeling he wasn't used to this kind of treatment. "I'm not the only one owed money," Albert added as he finished the transaction.

"So I've heard. How much do you think Zeke owed in all?"

"All told?" Albert pursed his lips. "Maybe about twenty grand?"

"Hell."

Regan's stomach tightened at the look on Mason's face. The number must be much higher than he'd expected.

"If you'd ever visited your uncle and great aunt, you'd know a little more about what's been going on. Zeke's been hitting up everyone for cash. He's a real nuisance." Albert handed him his receipt. Mason balled it up and stuffed it in his pocket.

"He was a nuisance, you mean. Now he's dead."

Mason's blunt words jolted Albert out of his diatribe. "I guess so, but he sure left a mess behind him."

"Well now I've started to clean it up." Mason grabbed the purchases that Susan had silently bagged up, and led the way back to his truck.

Regan followed him, climbing into the passenger seat. "Are you going to have enough money to pay everyone back?" she asked finally when the silence had stretched out too long.

Mason nodded curtly. "But things will be tight when I do."

CHAPTER FOURTEEN

SEVERAL HOURS LATER, Mason was finally calming down. If it hadn't been for Regan's presence, he'd have told Albert to shove his attitude up his ass and walked out without purchasing a single tool. Not that he didn't mean to honor Zeke's debts—of course he did—but he didn't need the likes of Albert Dundy acting like he was trying to pull a fast one.

In front of Regan, too. In front of the woman he was trying to convince to marry him. Some homecoming this was turning out to be. Who knew how many others felt like Albert did? Who knew how many would come around with their hands out before all was said and done? He'd had to hide his anger behind a façade of calm while he and Regan hit the building supply store to pick up a load of lumber and several spools of fencing wire, and then a furniture store to pick out a bed. Luckily, Zeke didn't seem to owe any money at either of those establishments. He'd decided to tackle the stables first and then the main barn. Once those were fixed up they'd have to face the task of fencing in the pastures. Mason had no idea how Regan would take to barbed wire and he wished he could call in some favors and get a few men to help, but the way he figured it, he couldn't ask anyone to help until he'd paid off Uncle Zeke's debts, and before he did that he needed to talk to his brothers. He'd scheduled a call for that evening.

One problem at a time, he told himself. At least he'd had a few hours out in the sunshine and fresh air to restore his mood. They were perched on two ladders resting side by side against the back wall of the stable, replacing an upper plank. Regan held the board in place while Mason fought to screw it in. Both of them worked at an unnatural angle with their arms over their heads. When Mason bobbled the screw and it bounced off of Regan's shoulder, he stifled a curse and reached for another. "Sorry," he called down.

"Watch it, Navy boy. I guess now I know why you made me wear these stupid safety glasses." Regan looked up at him and Mason had to smile. She looked adorable in them.

"I'll try to keep a better hold of the next one."

"You do that. And hurry—my arms are growing numb. I think they're going to get permanently stuck this way."

"I'm hurrying." So far she hadn't complained much about the hard work or the uncomfortable circumstances. The day was pleasant, at least, but they had many hours to go before they could check everything off their to-do list. Regan was far more cheerful than the SEALs he generally worked with. And nicer to look at, too.

Mason got the screw in the second time around and they climbed down their ladders and stood back to get a better look.

"Only forty more to go." Mason gave her bottom a squeeze.

Regan groaned. "I better get a prize when we're done."

"Oh, you will. I promise."

After dinner he left Regan making up their new bed and drove to Linda's Diner in town where he could get wi-fi. He connected the call to his brothers and filled them in on the news about Zeke's debts.

"Well, shit," Austin said. "That puts a dent in our capital."

"What do you want to do?" Zane asked.

"What can I do? I've got to pay everyone back. It'll take me days just to track all of them down—it's not like anyone kept a list—but when I find them, I'm going to pay them. What that means is I'll need each of you to wire me some cash. We've got all kinds of repairs to make on the place and then we'll need to purchase the livestock."

"I can do that." Austin was nodding. So was Zane.

Mason waited for Colt.

"Fine," he said finally. "I'll wire you some money. I just want it on record that I'm not getting anything out of this. First I'm supposed to find a wife, now I have to give you all my money? You know I plan to stay in the Air Force until I'm an old man."

"How's that wife business going?" He didn't have time for Colt's sob story.

All three shrugged and the familiar worry in Mason's gut grew stronger. "Well, what the hell are you all waiting for? Man up and get on it. None of you have any time to lose."

His brothers regarded him stonily.

"Calm down, Mase—you'll give yourself a heart attack," Zane finally said.

Calm down? "I'm the one dealing with all this bullshit. I'm the one with boots on the ground. The rest of you are out there farting around while I'm doing all the work!" He realized the restaurant had gone silent around him and he lowered his voice. "I need all of you to do your part. Are we clear?"

"You got it." Austin signed off, his expression as hard as iron.

"Will do," Zane said, "although I'd hardly call what we're doing farting around." He cut the call, too.

"I don't even want to get married," Colt started.

Mason slammed his laptop shut.

BY THE TIME they broke for dinner the following day, Regan knew all too well what Mason meant about not staying awake until eight. She was done in. Her arms and legs ached and she'd found muscles in places she'd never dreamed she'd had them. They had replaced all the missing or broken boards in the stable walls and fixed the stalls inside it. They raked out old bedding left from when Zeke still had horses and swept out the rest of the building, too. Regan turned her broom upside down and swept away as many of the cobwebs as she could reach. Once the shelves and storage areas were cleared of dust and debris, the building was back in working order. They worked quickly, not stopping to chat very often or to take many breaks. She soon realized that if she was tired, she had to speak up. Mason seemed able to work from morning to night without rest—and he seemed oblivious to her lesser capabilities.

He wasn't oblivious to her, however. Something he made sure to show her every chance he got.

Which she made sure was often.

He wasn't kidding when he said he tended to focus on the work at hand, though. Sometimes she didn't think he was aware of her at all—even if she was helping him. She was simply a pair of hands or eyes that supplemented his. Then he would come back to the present, notice her again and smile. She figured his time with the SEALs required that kind of concentration. It didn't bother her.

Much.

She was greedy for his attention, though. She wanted to chat with him about their plans and life and… everything. She wanted to hear about his time in the military, but when she brought it up, he shrugged it off, except to tell her the vaguest platitudes about the camaraderie he'd felt with his team and how honored he'd felt to serve his country. She knew those platitudes were true, but she also knew there had to be more. You didn't rise as far in the ranks of an elite military group like the SEALs without finding yourself in some tough places. She recognized that he wanted to shield her from all that—and that he might not want to probe too deeply into his years of service with someone who hadn't walked a similar path. Still, she wasn't some wilting daisy. She wanted to be Mason's partner. She hoped he knew he could depend on her when times got tough.

She loved talking to Mason. And touching him. Holding up boards while he screwed them in? It wasn't the same.

It was all too clear Mason was worried about the state of the Hall and Zeke's debts. Several men had stopped by in trucks in the time they were working. One or two had been curt, but the others had been cordial enough and welcomed her to Chance Creek politely. Still, sooner or later they gave an excuse to get Mason alone. After they drove away, Mason's mood grew grim.

She wished she could lighten his load, but all she could do was hold boards and hand him screws—and keep him company, whether they spoke or not. Last night he had made an effort to put his cares aside and pay attention to her. She knew it cost him to do so, and her love for him grew. He was a thoughtful man. An honorable one, too. He hadn't thought twice about paying his uncle's loans, even though it was putting him in a tenuous position.

"Why didn't Heloise pay off Zeke's debts?" she had asked him when they were getting ready for bed.

"I doubt she's aware of them. No one from these parts would approach an old lady and try to wring money from her."

"They don't have any problem approaching you."

"That's different. I'm a man in my prime with the ability to earn an income—not a woman in an assisted living situation. Besides, I've got the ranch. They figure I'll start earning again soon. Don't worry about it, honey. I'll see us through." He kissed her, but she could tell he was worried—very worried.

"Are you still going to ask your friends and neighbors for help?"

He turned onto his back and laced his hands behind his head. "I can't. Not now—not until I've set things right with everyone. You can understand that, can't you? I know it's making it rough on you and me, but…" He trailed off.

She understood. Mason's sense of honor was well developed. How could he put himself further into debt with the people his uncle owed money to?

"We'll get it all done—me and you." She climbed on top of him, straddling his waist. He put his hands on her thighs and traced them over her hips. "We can do anything together, can't we?"

"You are one in a million, Regan Anderson."

"You aren't half bad yourself, Mason Hall."

Midway through their second day they switched to the large barn. Just as before, they started by replacing planks of the exterior walls that had rotted out or broken off. Then they turned their attention to the loft.

"This is structural," Mason said with a frown. "We'll have to be careful how we fix it."

It took another quick trip to town and a lot of swearing to get new supports in place before they replaced the joists that had given up the ghost. Regan was impressed by Mason's careful workmanship—his desire to get things right. He was a stickler for safety, too—ordering her back when there was any danger.

Once the structural elements were solid, they began to cut boards to re-floor the loft. After a quick dinner—barely more than a sandwich eaten standing up near the truck—Regan reminded him she needed to go back to the Hall to wash up before her meeting. Mason nodded. "Go—rest a little if you can, first. You've worked hard." He gave her a long, lingering kiss. "Don't let Emma monopolize you too long, though. I'll be waiting for you."

"I bet you will."

When he mock growled at her, she shrieked and ran away. Mason gave chase, hooked her around the waist and toppled her to the ground, cushioning her fall, but straddling her just the same when she was down.

"Now I've got you."

"Yes, you have," she agreed happily. When he bent to ravish her, she gave herself up to it willingly and ten minutes later she was breathless, her clothing awry and her heart pounding. No one had ever affected her like

Mason did. Whenever he was close, every nerve in her body came alive, longing for him. She wouldn't stay long in town. Not with Mason waiting for her back at home. Not with a whole night ahead of them.

Or as much of a night as they could stay awake for.

Back at the hall, she took his advice, setting the alarm on her cell phone and lying down to rest after her shower. It was lucky she had the foresight to do so, because she was fast asleep on their new bed when it went off.

In town she easily located Linda's Diner, and when she went indoors, Emma was already there. She had a folder of paperwork in front of her that she slid across to Regan as soon as she sat down. A waitress appeared and took Regan's order, bringing her a cup of tea a moment later. Regan refused the offer of a slice of pie and opened the folder to take a look.

"Wow—a bakery?" she asked Emma when she'd scanned the first page. Emma nodded vigorously. "Have you ever managed a bakery before?"

"Yes—all through college, actually. I started out working the counter at a coffee shop in Billings where I went to school, but as soon as they figured out I'd show up to work at three-thirty in the morning consistently if that meant I could bake, they handed the whole operation over to me. I learned how to order supplies and set a menu. I know how to run the equipment and I've done all the food safety courses."

"That all sounds great. How much do you have for a deposit?"

Emma told her how much she'd saved, the cost of

the building she wanted and the estimate of her expenses for the first year. Regan quickly realized her numbers were right on the edge of acceptable. If she had any problems she might be in trouble.

"Do you think I should have waited until I had more money?" Emma asked in a small voice. "I know I'm cutting it thin."

"It would help if you had an emergency fund." Regan flipped through the paperwork again. "Wait a minute—the apartment above the shop has three bedrooms."

Emma nodded. "So?"

"So what about rental income? Do you have any friends who would move in with you? You could charge each of them two hundred and fifty dollars a month, and that extra five hundred a month could help pay your mortgage."

"I didn't even think of that."

They went over all Emma's numbers again, one at a time, and Regan was able to show her several adjustments that made her bottom line look more solid to the bank. At the end of their meeting, Emma was thrilled.

"That was so helpful. I feel like I have a shot now."

"I'm sure you do." Regan beamed at the compliment. "Good luck with your appointment. You'll have to let me know what happens."

"I will. Hey, I have a friend who's buying out an existing business and I know she could use some help, too. She wants to make some changes in the way they do things, so she needs to make a budget and find out how much she can spend up front. Could you help her with that?"

"Sure. Just have her call." Regan jotted down her cell phone number on a napkin.

Emma took it uncertainly. "You need to get some business cards made up."

"Oh, I don't know about that."

"I do. Get some made so I can spread the word about you. How are things going on the ranch?" She seemed more at ease now that they'd gone over her paperwork.

Regan wasn't sure how much to tell her. "I love the Hall, and I like working with Mason, but..."

"But what?"

"He's really worried. I'm sure you've heard about his uncle's debts."

Emma nodded. "I think everyone has."

"Well, it's just killing Mason. He's so proud he can't bear to have anyone think ill of him or his family. He wants to make sure he pays off every cent Zeke owes. Meanwhile, we're doing the best we can to fix the place up, but it's just the two of us." She shrugged helplessly. "It's slow going."

"I'll bet."

Regan decided it was time to turn the conversation to lighter topics and she didn't stay much longer, although she enjoyed the chance to chat with another woman. As she drove home, fighting to stay awake, she wondered if Emma was right. Maybe she had the start of a new business in her hands—one she could run right from the ranch.

CHAPTER FIFTEEN

BY THE TIME they were ready to tackle the pasture fencing a week later, Mason's worry had grown dangerously close to panic. He was pushing himself as hard as he could and there were still items on his checklist each day that didn't get done. Gone were the early morning lovemaking sessions with Regan. They got up as soon as the alarm went off. When it got dark, he brought Regan home over her protestations, ate a quick dinner with her, then went back out to accomplish anything else that could be done by flashlight. He showered and stumbled into bed when he simply couldn't move anymore, then got up to do it again the next day. Hardly twenty-four hours went by that he wasn't made aware of another of Zeke's debts. He'd paid the grocery store, the liquor store, several doctors and a dentist, a number of Zeke's friends, the fish and tackle store, and a grizzled old man who apparently kept Zeke's truck running. This wasn't the introduction to ranch life he'd wanted for Regan, but she was being a great sport. He tried to do everything he could to show her his appreciation. She was a great sport about that as well.

Still, if they didn't get a move on, they would lose this chance to inherit the ranch. If only Austin could get home sooner, they'd be able to work at twice the pace. Regan was amazing, but she struggled to keep up with him. Zeke's damn debts had put him in an untenable position—a work party or two would have given him a leg up on his lists, but with only Regan to help him, he was losing ground fast.

He knew they'd have to do the best they could and trust that things would work out. He'd thought about asking Heloise to back off on her outrageous deadlines. Instinct told him not to do so, however. He was in her favor now, but she could just as easily change her mind and leave the Hall to Darren or one of his kids. At the end of the day, Mason didn't care about the money—he cared about the land.

Which was all well and good, except he needed more money. Which meant another uncomfortable call to his brothers. While Regan puttered in the kitchen getting her breakfast, he set up his laptop in the bedroom so she wouldn't hear the gist of their conversation. They'd gotten an internet connection installed to the Hall finally, so at least he no longer needed to run to town. When all three of his brothers were connected, he gave them an update on the state of things.

"This could bankrupt us, you know," Zane said when he was done.

"Heloise said she'd return the money to us if we

failed to get the ranch up and running. Eventually." He didn't mention the circumstances in which they'd get it.

"Meanwhile, we'll have given everything we've got to the place and Darren will make off with it in the end."

"It isn't going to come to that. Not if each of us does what he's supposed to do."

No one answered that and Mason could see that none of them had made any progress on finding a wife. "For God's sake, if I can find a woman the rest of you can, too."

"Do you know how I'm spending my days?" Austin said, his face filling the screen. "Getting shot at. In case you forgot, the three of us are still fighting for our country while you romp in the hay with your girl-friend."

"I'm not romping." Not as often as he wanted to, anyway. "Besides, Colt's not fighting for his country. He's in Florida, for crying out loud. There's all kinds of women in Florida."

"Not any I want to marry." Colt drawled out his words.

"Are you going to send the damn money or not?" Mason had had enough of the conversation.

"We'll send it." Austin's tone was still hard. "But you'd better watch every penny and you'd better hold up your end. Just because you've got a girl playing house with you in the Hall doesn't mean you're any closer to marriage than we are. And you're no damn closer to having a baby. If you don't step it up, then we're throwing our cash down a rathole!"

"Are you calling the Hall a rathole?"

Austin cut the connection.

"You'd better back off, Mason." Zane was giving him a hard look. "Things are pretty tense over here just now. Austin's unit has had it tough."

"Well it ain't no picnic here, either."

"No one's shooting at you, are they?" That was Colt.

"No." Of course not. They were right—he was blowing this out of proportion. He didn't seem to be able to keep things in proportion these days.

"Look, I know you're carrying the brunt of Heloise's craziness. I know it's tough—you love that place, just like I do." Zane held his gaze. "So get the mission done. Whatever it takes."

Mason nodded, shame welling up in his chest, an uncomfortable feeling he wasn't used to. His brothers were right; he was panicking like a raw recruit. He could get this done. He had to. "You're right. I'll handle it. You guys just stay safe and get on home. With wives."

He cut the connection, too.

Two hours later, after another trip to town, he and Regan set out with spools of wire and all the tools they'd need in the back of the truck he'd bought second-hand from a dealership in town. They'd spent the previous day shoring up the fence posts. Today they had to attach the wire. They could have walked to the closest pasture, but by the end of the day they'd cover a lot of ground and the spools, especially, were heavy. They'd need the vehicle throughout the process.

The day was overcast and Mason hoped the rain would hold off, as the weatherman had predicted. He hadn't allotted time for bad weather. He couldn't. He handed Regan a pair of work gloves, lifted a spool of plain wire out of the back of the truck and brought it to the corner post. He showed Regan how to start off by wrapping the end of the wire around the post several times before tying it off to itself. Together they picked up the rod that went through the large spool of wire and walked down the length of the pasture to the next wooden post, letting the wire play out behind them.

In between the sturdy wooden posts were smaller metal ones to hold up the wire and give the fence more structure. Once the wire was strung between the wooden ones, Mason demonstrated how to use a small come-along to pull it tight. "Not too tight," he cautioned her, showing her how much play to leave in the line as he cranked it. "Now comes the fun part."

The wire had to be tied to each metal post along the length of the side of the pasture. A time-consuming, annoying task, it was all too easy to tear up your gloves—and your hands—on the sharp metal ties. The small lengths of metal hooked around the wire on one side of the metal bars, bent around to the other side of the support, and needed to be wrapped around the wire again with a pair of pliers. Once he'd shown Regan how it was done, he handed her a bag of ties and her own pair of pliers and set her to work. He walked to the far end of the field to work his way back to her. When he glanced over his shoulder, she was hard at it. She was a hell of a woman. He wished he was showing her a better time. They hadn't even made love in the last few days.

Time to lighten things up, even if only for a moment. "Race you," he called. "Winner gets to feel up the loser." He was rewarded with a smile from Regan, but he had to work hard to feel like playing games. He told himself his father wouldn't have succumbed to worry like he was, but the thought of his balance sheet sinking like a stone through pond water made it hard to think of anything else.

"That game seems stacked against me," Regan called back, already hard at work.

"Do you mind?"

"Not really."

She was right; he moved far faster than she did since he had more experience and stronger muscles in his hands and arms. He had the goad of knowing his dream was slipping through his fingers, too. Once in a while he heard a muffled oath and knew her pliers had slipped or she'd dropped a tie. When he glanced her way, she was working quickly.

"I'm going to beat you!" she said when she saw him looking.

"I doubt it." When he passed the halfway mark, he shook off his dark thoughts, threw down his pliers, strode over to her and lifted her right off the ground, spinning her in a circle. He set her down, slid his hands up under her shirt and bra, and caressed her breasts until they tightened into stiff peaks. He growled low in his throat. "I should have said the winner gets to do more than feel up the loser."

"We've got work to do. Lots of it. Time for playing tonight when we're done." She knocked the cowboy hat he wore today low down over his nose.

"Hey." He cocked it back and stole a kiss. "All right, but you'd better be ready for some serious action tonight."

"Don't worry—I will be." But Regan wasn't paying attention to him anymore. "Who is that?"

He turned to see a dark green Chevy truck rumbling down the track that led to the pastures. Whoever it was must have stopped at the house first, found it empty and decided to come looking for them. His heart sank again. Anyone that determined had to have bad news. He released her and she smoothed her clothing back into place.

"I don't recognize the truck."

They waited until it rumbled down the worn track and came to a stop nearby. An old man climbed out stiffly and made his way to them.

"Hello," he said. "I don't suppose you recognize me."

Mason wracked his memory. "Allen James?"

"That's right!" The old man chuckled. "I was friends with your grandfather. Used to stop by to shoot the breeze with him when you were just a little thing."

"Nice to see you again, Allen. What can I do for

you? Did you come to get a look at the place? We're doing our best to fix it up." So Zeke owed Allen money too. Was there no end to the creditors he needed to pay off? How much would it be this time? Two hundred dollars? Two thousand? Shame washed over him on behalf of his uncle. Allen James had been like a brother to Zeke's father, Abraham Hall. They'd grown up together.

"Your father would be proud of you for what you're doing. Everyone's been saying what a shame it was that Zeke let the place go like he did. I'm glad you're putting things back to rights. The county wouldn't be the same without the Hall."

"Thank you."

"Well, I won't take up much more of your time. I just wanted to give you this." He handed an envelope to Mason.

"What is it?" A bill?

"I heard about the way you've been going around town making good on Zeke's debts. Made me happy to know how well you'd turned out. Your grandfather was always an honorable man. So was your father. I miss them both. When Abe died I lost a good friend." The old man swallowed. "I owed him a little money at the time, too. Just a little, mind you. We'd gone out fishing one day, stopped at the bar on the way home. I'd left my wallet in the truck and he covered my tab. Forgot all about it until it was too late." Allen looked away for a moment and Mason knew the past had enveloped him. "It's always bugged me a little I didn't settle my debt with him before he passed. Now I've settled it with you." He patted the envelope in Mason's hand. "I'll be on my way now, but I'll be back from time to time to check in on you. It's good to see a Hall in the Hall again." He smiled at his own small joke and made his way slowly back to the truck.

When he was gone, Mason opened the envelope and pulled out eighteen dollars and fifty-two cents. For one moment he felt as if his father was at his side, sharing the joke. Sharing the warm feeling that came from knowing that someone believed in you, even if you were fast losing faith in yourself.

Eighteen dollars and fifty-two cents didn't put a dent in the amount of money he'd already spent on the ranch, but the gesture meant more to him than all the gold in the treasury could have. He was home—back to a place where honor mattered. Where family mattered. Where the Halls had always lived in the Hall.

He turned to Regan, saw tears sparkling in her eyes and was almost undone by the emotion that assailed him.

He would restore the Hall. He would restore his family. He would be the man that Regan deserved.

That's it, son. You've got this. He heard his father's voice in his mind. Felt the pat of his hand on his shoulder, like he used to do when times got tough.

He swore he wouldn't let his father down.

"Let's have lunch. Then we'll get back to work."

Regan nodded and they ate the lunch they'd packed on the tailgate of the truck. Afterward, they moved back to the task of tying the wire to the uprights. Energized by Allen's visit, Mason found himself moving faster, getting the job done with efficiency and speed. Once he'd helped Regan finish her part of the fence, they repeated the process of spooling out the wire and attaching it to the uprights several times. The clouds got more ominous as the afternoon progressed. When they took another break for dinner, Mason squinted up at them.

"I'm not sure our luck is going to hold. If we see lightning, we'll have to call it quits. Otherwise I intend to work through it. Are you up for that?"

Regan nodded. "Of course." She finished up her sandwich, gulped down a few swallows of water. "Let's get back to work, then. No more fooling around."

"Damn, I like fooling around." But she was right. It was time to get serious. Stringing the barbed wire at the top of the fence was going to be the biggest pain of all. Doing it in the rain would be even worse. The prospect didn't faze him, though—not as pumped as he was to conquer this obstacle.

A half-hour later, the rain came, at first in scattered drops, but quickly increasing to a steady shower.

"Grab our jackets." Mason gestured toward the truck as he tightened the come-along on the wire he was installing. Regan raced off to fetch them and was back in a moment. Mason was glad he'd had the foresight to bring them along.

The rain picked up its pace as they fastened the wire to the posts and tied the individual metal ties. It took longer now that everything was slick. Mason sped up his motions as best he could, but Regan was slowing down as evening drew in.

"Just the barbed wire to do now." He'd had them string all the plain wires around the entire pasture first, saving the barbed wire to do all at once. "We have to be even more careful now, okay? Gloves on all the time."

Regan nodded. Strands of her auburn hair had straggled out of the practical ponytail she wore. Water dripped down from them onto the collar of her raincoat. She looked small and serious. Mason longed to take her home and warm her before a fire, but he wasn't going to quit until they finished this pasture. It had become a milestone to him in almost a superstitious manner. If they completed it, then they could do anything else that the ranch threw at them. If not—well, he didn't want to consider that. Once more they approached a corner post. The barbed wire went above all the others on the fence, so Mason looped it around up high and attached the staples that held it in place. This spool was heavier than the others had been and Regan staggered as they walked the length of the pasture to the next wooden post.

"You can do it," he cheered her on.

"I know." But Mason heard the strain in her voice. They were long past joking around with each other now. As the day had lengthened, all conversation and kidding around had stopped. Now they had to save all their strength for the work at hand. Regan was breathing hard by the time they put the spool down and she looked thoroughly spent. He eyed her warily and took over without a word, looping this end and attaching the come-along. Once the wire was tight enough, they moved along its length again, attaching the ties. Regan was lagging far behind by the time they were done. Mason didn't blame her; the rain made a difficult job even harder and she was tired, but he also knew they needed to kick up the pace or they'd run out of daylight.

In the distance, thunder rumbled.

Regan's gaze met his. "We'd better head back to the house. We can finish this up tomorrow."

Mason shook his head. "You go. I'm staying and finishing this today."

"Mason—"

"I said I'm staying." Her eyes widened at his sharp tone, and he was instantly sorry. "Honey, I have to." He willed her to understand. He couldn't give up now. If he did, he didn't know how they'd catch up again.

After a long moment, she nodded and got back to work.

"You should go back to the Hall. I can do the rest myself."

"If you're staying, I'm staying."

"Then let's get going."

THEY WERE OUT of their minds working on a metal fence in the middle of a thunderstorm, but she refused to leave Mason's side—not when he'd half worked himself to death already. Night after night he'd gone back to work after bringing her home and grabbing a quick bite to eat. Even when she could barely walk up the stairs to their bedroom, he'd worked long into the night until the whole ranch was pitch black except the tiny pinprick of his flashlight. He was up again at dawn. She didn't know how he remained on his feet.

With the rain falling harder and thunder rumbling in the distance there was no way she'd leave him alone now. Her only hope was to work fast enough to know they'd get the job done before the lightning came close. Mason attached the wire to the corner post and they started down another length of the pasture, trailing out the barbed wire from the spool they carried between them.

"As soon as we're done we'll get a hot bath and a good meal," Mason said.

"Great." She squinted as the rain fell in sheets around her, stumbling in the mud as they went. This was beyond ridiculous—this was crazy. Thunder rumbled again. A flash of light far off in the distance caught her eye.

They reached the far end and she waited for him to attach the wire to the corner post and use the come-along to tighten it. Then it was back to tying the barbed wire to the metal uprights in between.

She worked as fast as she could, but the rain made her fingers clumsy and it was difficult to attach the little pieces of metal to the wire and poles. When she dropped her pliers twice in a row, she swore and had to take deep breaths to keep from chucking them into the next field.

Mason, on the other hand, seemed to be catching a second wind. He nearly vibrated with energy as he worked down the line, and she wondered if this crisis reminded him of his time with the SEALs. Maybe life on the ranch had been too slow and easy for him. Maybe he needed the adrenaline of a tense situation to get him through the day. As they tied the barbed wire to the uprights, the storm moved closer, until she could count the seconds between the flashes of light and the roar of thunder.

When they finished the second side of the pasture, she went to help him with the spool of wire again. Just like before, he looped one end around the wooden corner post and stapled it on tight. She couldn't believe he meant to continue working with the storm nearly overhead.

"Mason, we have to go!"

"We're nearly done. Go on—I can do the rest myself." He turned back to the work before she could protest and there was nothing for it but to follow his lead. In another moment they were hobbling down the slick muddy pasture to the third wooden post. Not an inch of her was dry anymore. Her hair straggled into her eyes and water streamed down her neck into her clothing. She was cold, tired and every muscle in her body ached. When they reached the far end, she dropped her side of the spool. A bolt of lightning zigzagged across the sky and fractured it into pieces. The thunder that followed on its heels shook the ground beneath her feet.

Mason had attached the come-along and was cranking it like a madman, tightening the wire until it went taut.

"Go home," he bellowed over his shoulder. "Get back to the Hall."

"You have to come too!"

"The storm will be past in a minute—I'll be fine!"

Another stab of lightening split the sky. Thunder roared over their heads.

"God damn it, Mason! We've got to go!"

He gave the come-along another few violent cranks. "Go, Regan—I'll be right there!"

"Mason!"

He cranked it one last time just as she ran to his side and grabbed his arm. The wire snapped with a sound like a whip cracking—the end skimming by barely an inch from both their faces. Regan shrieked. The come-along clattered against the fence post.

Mason stood stock still—his arms outstretched to shield her—his face blank with shock.

Regan stared back at him, all too aware of how close both of them had just come to being hurt.

"Regan—"

She knew what he meant to say—knew this moment would etch in his mind forevermore. Knew that as single-mindedly as he'd just tried to finish the job, he'd never meant to hurt her. Never meant to put her in danger.

But he had.

Regan began to sob in a delayed reaction to her fear. She was so tired. So overwhelmed. She tried to scrub the tears from her face but they kept on coming. "I'm sorry. I'm fine," she babbled, but Mason still stared at her, as if seeing her for the first time in days.

She used her sleeve to wipe her eyes, then laughed at the impossibility of it. She was soaked through. Not one inch dry enough to dry anything else. Her laughter turned into another sob.

To her horror, Mason's knees buckled and he sank into the mud.

"Mason—" She lunged for him.

He held up a hand to fend her off. "That wire could have sliced you to the bone. Jesus—it could have killed you."

"But it didn't. I'm fine." She pushed her hair roughly out of her eyes. Mason's face was twisted in anguish and she knew him well enough that he'd blame himself for the accident. The rain continued to bucket down, but she didn't care anymore. The only thing that mattered to her was getting that expression off of Mason's face.

"What the hell am I doing?"

She knew he was referring to more than their current working conditions. Above them, lightning flashed again and thunder shook the ground beneath her feet. "We can do this. Even if we don't finish the fence today, we can still do this." Helplessness filled her as she saw the impossibility of their task overwhelming Mason. She couldn't stand the pain etched on his features.

"No, we can't." He was shaking his head. He was in shock, she knew it. Knew too that this day of reckoning had probably been a long time coming. Mason was fresh out of the military. Fresh out of a war zone, for heaven's sake. He'd made the transition home so seamlessly until now. Was it any surprise that it would all come crashing down?

"Let's get you home. Let's get you dry."

"You go." He braced his palms on his thighs, his shoulders hunching. The rain streamed down over him. Over her, too. There was no way she was leaving him like this—all but drowning on solid ground.

She fell to her knees in front of him. "We'll work harder tomorrow. Faster. When the rain's gone. We'll get it done."

"It isn't just the fence." Lightning shot across the sky again, revealing his hollow eyes and taut face, but the pause before the thunder came was longer than before. The storm was already passing.

"Then what is it? Tell me—I can help."

He shook his head again. "You asked me once what my nickname was. I didn't want to tell you. I didn't want you to know what I could be like."

"I don't understand. What is it?" She was frightened for him. She'd never seen him like this, full of shame and self-loathing.

"Straightshot. It's because of the way I accomplish

missions." His voice was rough. "Because of the way I always know the fastest way to get from here to there. To get things done. Give me any objective and I'll tell you exactly how to accomplish it. Whether or not it can be accomplished. I'm always right." He broke off. She could hear his ragged breathing. "It worked—in the Navy it worked. I got things done. I got the men through, we did what we had to and we got out again. Alive. I bullied them, hounded them, taunted them—pushed them to the edge of their limits. Whatever it took to keep them moving when things got tough. Their lives depended on it. Sometimes they wanted to give up and die. I couldn't let them. I didn't let them. I did anything—said anything—I had to do or say to keep them going. I was good at finding the shortest distance from start to done. The best. But now—"

Regan's eyes filled again as his voice cracked. She knew what he meant to say. That he'd left behind the world he knew. That what made him a star in the military didn't work here on the ranch. It didn't work with her.

"If I'd lost you—because I fucked up—"

"You didn't lose me. You're not going to lose me." What could she say to stop him from losing faith?

"Yes, I am." He paused, hands braced on his thighs, his head bowed. "Regan, I did something." He turned a hopeless gaze on her and she went cold.

What had he done? The thunder and lightning were farther away now, the rain beginning to taper off.

"I didn't tell you everything. Heloise has more

conditions."

She started breathing again. This she could handle. She touched his shoulder, felt his muscles hard and cold beneath his wet jacket and shirt. Nothing he could say about Heloise would change her mind about the way she felt about him. "What are they?"

"Austin, Zane, Colt and I—we all have to get married within the year."

Regan blinked. The wife wanted ad. Now it made perfect sense. "Okay, so you needed to meet someone fast and you placed an ad. So what? I wouldn't have met you if you hadn't."

"There's more."

"Tell me." She wanted to take him into her arms and tell him all was well, but she sensed he wouldn't accept that comfort. Not until he'd come clean.

"We have to have a baby. Before the year is up. That's why I've been pushing so hard. That's why I rushed you into this."

She heard the self-reproach in his voice, but that wasn't why she pulled back. "You don't love me? Tell me right now if you don't love me, Mason Hall!"

"Of course I love you." His lethargy fell away as his gaze snapped to hers and he cupped her face in his cold hands. "Regan, honey—" He didn't waste time on words. He kissed her, and as thunder rumbled again in the distance, Regan leaned into his kiss, tasting all that was sweet about Mason, all that she craved.

Of course he loved her. She knew that better than she knew her own name, but—

"You don't want a child?" She pulled away to ask the question.

"I'll give you a child right now if that's what you want. Anything to be with you."

It was almost enough. Almost.

"You have to want it too."

He sank back, letting her go. "I don't know how to be a father. I don't know how to be a husband. Look at me." He rose to his feet and tugged her up, too. Their pants were coated with mud, their clothing soaked. "How can I get you pregnant when I don't even know if we'll have a place to live?" He surveyed the fence, the barbed wire slack by their feet. She could tell all his late nights and early mornings had caught up with him. The strain of paying Zeke's debts and watching his careful budget fall apart. Mason was only a man.

The rain began to tail off as the thunder receded. "Are you afraid your brothers won't marry?"

"I don't know. And I don't know if we can get the ranch ready in time for the cattle we need to have. What if we don't make it? We could do everything right and still lose it all if Colt doesn't come through."

Now she understood why he wanted Colt to come home so badly. She let his words sink in. If she married Mason, there were no guarantees. They could end up pregnant and penniless.

Well, not penniless.

Regan realized she'd been holding back. Even though she thought she wanted to marry Mason, she hadn't committed to him or to the ranch all the way.

But now she was ready to. She'd never find a man she loved more than him, and she'd never find a man more dedicated to his home and family. Mason thought more about those topics than any man she'd ever met. It was time for her to put her money where her mouth was and meet him halfway.

"We'll get the ranch ready in time," she assured him. "And we'll make those brothers of yours get married. We can do this, Mason. I know we can. And if we blow all of your money trying, there's always mine. I have savings, too. And I have my weenie apartment—at least for now. In a pinch, I could get my old job back." She let her lips curve up, hoping he got the joke.

He shook his head. "Why don't you hate me?"

She reached up to plant a kiss on the corner of his mouth. "Because I love you too much. I don't need a ranch, Mason. I don't need a big, old mansion, either. All I need is you. We'll make a home for ourselves wherever we go."

He was silent a long moment, searching her face as if trying to decide whether she was speaking the truth. "I don't deserve you."

"Yes, you do. Let's go home."

She held her breath while he surveyed the soaking pasture, the snapped wire and the storm clouds dissipating overhead. "You go on. I need to take a walk. I need to clear my head."

Regan peered at him worriedly. She obviously hadn't convinced him. But Mason deserved to make up his own mind about what to do next. "Come get changed first. Then take all the time you need."

"Okay." They walked back to the Hall in silence, leaving the truck and the tools behind to retrieve in the morning. Regan's concern grew with every step. Mason was quiet—too quiet. He changed swiftly, leaving his wet things in the bathroom draped over the tub, and kissed her before leaving again through the back door, but she could almost feel him wrestling with his inner demons. Regan trailed him into the kitchen to watch him go.

"Don't wait up." Shoving his hands in his pockets, he headed down the track toward the creek.

Regan's heart broke for him as she watched him walk away.

WHEN MASON REACHED Chance Creek, the storm clouds were breaking up and the last rays of the sun colored the flowing water a deep orange-gold. He paced the banks, sorting through his tangled thoughts. He wanted Regan more than he ever had—was sure she was the one he was meant to spend his life with.

But not on the ranch.

He finally let his brothers' protests sink in. He'd been pushing all of them to conform to his dream of reestablishing his family here where they'd always lived. They'd tried to tell him the terms were too rough.

He hadn't listened.

Austin and Zane loved the place as much as he did, but neither of them wanted to rush settling down. Colt didn't even want to get married—or return to the ranch, for that matter. Why should everyone around him be miserable just so he got what he wanted?

And why should he risk Regan's future—and the future of any children they might have—on a hurried trip to the altar and the chance that his brothers wouldn't come through?

It was time to give up Crescent Hall—as much as it cost him to admit it. Time to figure out another way to make a living so he could afford a wife and family. He'd still marry Regan—if she'd have him—but first he'd make sure he could provide for her. They'd have a long engagement, and they wouldn't start a family for a while, but they'd get there.

Somehow.

As the dusk bled into dark, Mason turned around and headed toward home. He was nearly undone again when he saw the lights of the Hall blazing forth. Welcoming him back. Giving up his home a second time would be hard to take. But he'd still have Regan, and that was more than enough.

Once again as he walked heavily toward the Hall he felt his father's presence beside him. He got no flashes of insight—no fatherly messages from beyond. Just a sense that he wasn't alone in this dark hour.

He paused at the back door, not wanting to break the spell of the night. His heart was heavy with the knowledge that they'd have to leave, but he was comforted by the thought that he was finally doing the right thing. Being honest with himself—and with

Regan—about what his capabilities truly were.

She met him in the kitchen where she must have been waiting for him. Rising to her feet from the kitchen table where she'd been sitting in the dark, she crossed the room swiftly and threw herself into his arms.

"Don't say we can't be together." She hugged him close and her cheek was damp against his throat.

"We can be together, sweetheart. Just not here."

REGAN LISTENED QUIETLY to all of Mason's reasons for not going ahead with trying to secure the ranch. She let him tick off on his fingers all the ways they'd be putting their own future in jeopardy by investing their time and money into a project whose outcome they couldn't control. She waited while he told her he meant to find a job and then try to buy a small property on the outskirts of town where they could keep a couple of horses and participate in country life even if they couldn't ranch. He promised her he would marry her as soon as he had his own situation in order. He hoped she could wait for him, but understood if she couldn't.

Long after he'd fallen into an exhausted slumber in their bed in the tower room, Regan stayed awake, thinking their situation over. Mason was right—it was risky going ahead with the plan to secure the ranch if Austin, Zane and Colt weren't on board, but the more she thought about it, the more every fiber of her being rebelled against the idea of leaving Crescent Hall behind.

She slipped out of bed, found Mason's laptop and tip-toed downstairs to the kitchen, where she propped it open on the table and turned it on. Bringing up Skype, she easily found his brothers in his list of contacts and started a four-way call.

Colt was the first to answer. He hunched down to look at her, his eyebrows shooting up. "Mason, you've changed." He grinned and she grinned back.

"I needed to talk to you and your brothers. I'm Regan, by the way."

"I figured as much."

"What's going on?" Austin had come online. Like Colt, he was peering at her.

"It's about Mason."

"Is he okay?" When Zane came on she breathed a sigh of relief. She'd only get one chance at this. Now she had all three of them listening.

"Mason's okay, but you three need to know what's going on. He's decided to give up."

"Give up? Mason?"

She understood Zane's disbelief.

"Because of me. I need you to help me stop him."

"You'd better start at the beginning." That was Austin. Regan took a deep breath and did just that. She told them all about what they'd found when they got to Crescent Hall, how they'd been determined to fix everything and planned to ask for help from friends and neighbors. She told them about Zeke's debts and the way Mason didn't feel he could approach anyone for aid until he'd paid them all off. She knew they'd heard it all before, but she wanted them to truly understand it before she went on to explain how hard he'd been pushing himself and how she'd tried to help. How today they'd worked through the thunderstorm until the wire snapped—and then Mason had snapped, too.

"Shit—no one was hurt?" Austin interjected.

"No. Missed us by less than an inch, though."

Colt whistled. "I can see why he got upset."

"He's more than upset. He's given up. He says that even if we do everything right—get married, get pregnant, get the ranch up and running, there's no guarantee you guys will do your part. So he doesn't even want to try."

All three men were silent.

At last Zane said, "You're all right with the rest of it? Getting hitched to Mason? Having a kid?"

Her cheeks warmed, but she nodded. "I can't think of anything I'd rather do."

"I'll be home in less than two months. If you two can hold the fort until then I'll work like crazy to help you get the place set up in time. I've been answering some of the messages from the wife wanted ad. Nothing's stuck so far, but I'll keep trying."

Zane nodded. "I want Crescent Hall back in the family. Mason knows that. I won't be out of the service until fall, but there's nothing I'd rather do than get back to ranching."

"What about getting married?"

"Hell, I don't have anything against that, either. Just haven't found the right one yet. It's hard when I'm over here."

"But you'll try?"

"I'll more than try. I'll guarantee it."

"So that leaves me," Colt said after another silence.

"That leaves you," Regan said. "You don't have to do it, but if you're not going to, you have to tell us right now. It isn't fair to let the rest of us invest time and money if you don't intend to follow through."

"I know." Colt scratched the back of his neck. "I just... never thought about getting hitched yet. Not until Mason started all this."

"Say the word and we'll call the whole thing off," Regan said. "No one will blame you."

"Hell." Colt made a face. "Don't call it off. I'll do it."

"You swear?" Austin leaned into the screen. "You'll put Mason into a hell of a fix if you screw this up."

"I swear!"

"All right, then. Everyone is on the same page? You all promise to get married if we get the ranch set up and stock it with cattle?"

The men nodded. Even Colt.

"But you said Mason had given up. How are you going to change his mind?" Austin asked.

"Oh, I've got a few tricks up my sleeves."

MASON WOKE TO the smell of bacon frying and a bright, clear blue sky outside his window. For one moment his heart lifted at the thought of being at home on the ranch with a pretty woman cooking breakfast for him.

Then he remembered the events of the previous day. He'd nearly hurt Regan with his single-minded pursuit of the ranch.

He'd decided to give it up for good.

Soon he'd leave the Hall again and with it all the sweet memories of waking up next to Regan, working with her, playing with her—building a life together.

No, he'd still have that. Just somewhere else. Somewhere new. There was nothing to say it wouldn't be as sweet. Maybe it would turn out to be better.

Mason snorted, not believing that for an instant, but he made himself get out of bed and dressed in his work clothes, although he didn't think he'd be doing any more work. First he'd get in touch with his brothers and let them know what was happening. Then he'd sit down with Regan and plan what to do next. At some point he'd let Heloise know it was time to turn the Hall over to Darren.

His fingers clenched themselves into fists.

He found Regan in the kitchen humming a light tune as she forked the bacon out of the pan onto a plate lined with paper towels. She was dressed in a t-shirt and jeans shorts this morning. He hadn't seen her in shorts before. She looked good.

"Morning." She came to give him a peck on the

cheek.

"Morning." Mason frowned. What was she so happy about?

"Have some breakfast and we'll talk."

"Okay."

He sat where she indicated and ate what she put on his plate, as if he was back in the service. The meal was well-prepared, but he couldn't have said what it was he swallowed. She poured him a cup of coffee and another for herself, then sat across from him.

"We're not giving up."

"Regan—"

"Hear me out." She traced a finger around the brim of the cup. "I love you. I'll love you even if we end up in an apartment working for minimum wage. But we've got a chance for something better here."

"Emphasis on the word *chance*." But his heart quickened its pace. What was she suggesting?

"I talked to your brothers last night." His eyebrows shot up at this news. "They promised me they'd get married in time. All three of them."

"Even Colt?"

"Even Colt. I'm willing to take a chance. I want to marry you. I want a child—I told you that right from the beginning. I know we can do what it takes to make this ranch a going concern."

"I wish I was as sure as you are."

"We can do it. I know we can. You just have to have a little faith."

Mason wanted to believe her. He wanted to have

that faith, but he knew that if they failed he'd be consigning her to years of hard work to regain their current position. His savings weren't that large—they could easily be eaten up trying to stock the ranch with cattle, aside from all the repairs.

"Like I said yesterday, if we blow all your saving on the ranch, we'll still have mine. We can use my money to start over." Her eyes pleaded with him to say yes.

He shook his head. "I won't spend your savings under any condition."

"Then we'll get jobs. We'll start small. Heck, we can move into my parents' basement for a few months if times get really tough."

He was shaking his head again. "This has to end right now. When I marry you, my first responsibility is to take care of my family—you and any children we have. It makes far more sense to cut our losses now and start fresh."

She practically groaned. "Even if I want to stay right here? I'm not marrying you for your looks, sailor—it's the Hall I'm after."

Mason felt his lips twitch. "You'd put up with me just to get my house?"

"Damn straight. It's a hell of a house." She pushed her plate away, came around the table and sat on his lap. "Can we stay? Pretty please?"

It was a tempting offer, but he resisted. "It's not the prudent thing to do. I'm sorry, honey."

She hopped off again. "Not good enough." She took his hand and tugged him to his feet.

"Where are we going?"

She led him out the back door and across the yard that was still damp from the previous evening's rain. "To settle this argument the Hall way. We're going to run the Course."

"We're going to what?" He stopped in his tracks, but she tugged him forward.

"Run the Course. Winner takes all. If you beat me, we'll leave Crescent Hall and go live in my apartment. If I win, we'll stay here and do our damnedest to beat Heloise's deadline."

He grinned despite himself at the thought of Regan running the Course. "You don't have a chance in hell of winning."

"Oh yeah? Watch me, Navy boy."

They reached the woods and took their places at the starting line.

"Take off your shirt," Regan commanded him. He did as he was told, grateful to know she still found him attractive—could still joke around even in a situation as difficult as this.

"You ready?"

"Almost." She stripped off hers as well, unhooking her bra and tossing it away as well.

"Wait—hold up. That's not—"

"Onyourmark, getset, go!" She shouted in one long rush and sprinted off toward the monkey bars.

Mason could only stand and gape.

SO FAR HER plan was working. She was halfway across the monkey bars before footsteps behind her told her Mason had gotten over his shock and was trying to catch up. She might not be in the military, but she'd been an expert at this type of playground equipment back in elementary school. She flung one hand after the next and leaped off it before Mason reached the bars at all.

She broke into another run, charging toward the climbing wall for all she was worth. Running without a bra wasn't very comfortable, so she clamped one arm across her chest and fought to hold the girls in place. There were no footholds here, no climbing aids for the vertically impaired. As the wall loomed closer, she wondered how Mason and his brothers had made it over when they were kids. Probably just jumped for the top, she thought as she closed her eyes and hurled herself up.

She slammed into the wooden wall and fell back into the dirt. Mason shouted behind her, raced to her side, and crouched down beside her.

"Are you okay?"

Taking advantage of his concern, she sprang to her feet, set one sneaker on his thigh, pushed off and grabbed the top of the wall. She swung her leg up, missed the top by nearly a foot, swung back and tried again. This time she got closer, but not close enough. Her arms were tiring fast. She was about to lose her grip.

Hands on her ass nearly made her let go, but Mason boosted her up and over before she had time to object. She hit the ground hard on the other side and was still staggering, dazed, when he leaped down beside her.

"Sweetheart. You're going to hurt yourself."

She pushed him away again and raced onward. If she could keep him off-balance she might just win this thing. And she needed to win it. For his dreams. For their children. For the sake of all of them.

The tires. She could do these.

It took all her concentration, though, to keep her footing. She wiped her face with her arm and picked up speed as she went. The army crawl obstacle had her swearing as dirt smeared all over her bare chest and shorts. Sticks and leaves poked and scratched her, and she was beginning to wish she'd kept her top on after all, but although annoying, the obstacle wasn't hard. Next, she managed to traverse a gully on a rope swing and time her leap off it to land on the opposite side.

When she reached the log balance beams, however, she came up short.

"Regan," Mason said as he jogged up behind her. She knew he wasn't giving it his all—that was obvious. He'd have left her far behind if he had. But she didn't care. If it took her bobbing breasts to convince him to give saving the ranch another chance, then so be it. The rules of this game were changing even as they played it. All she had to do was cross the finish line first.

By any means necessary.

The angled logs, which had scared her from a distance, were even more frightening up close. They were too wide and slick to shimmy up. Running at them full tilt was the only way to reach the top. Regan backed up, took a deep breath and raced for the nearest one. She saw Mason's worried expression, saw him reach his hands out to catch her should she fall, then her full attention was on the log itself.

Her momentum carried her halfway up and she kept moving, knowing if she stopped she'd slide right back down. She pitched forward as her feet lost their grip, and as she fell she caught the top of the log and held on for dear life.

Once more Mason came to her aid. He held a hand beneath the bottom of one of her feet, giving her just enough traction to push up and onto the horizontal log that formed the balance beam itself. Sitting on one end of it, legs dangling to either side, she caught her breath.

And realized this obstacle was all but impossible.

The log was thick, but not thick enough to make the crossing comfortable. Balance had never been her strong suit. There was no way she could stand up and walk along the log, let alone move along it as fast as Mason had.

"You can cross it just as you are," Mason said in a conversational tone. "That's how we all started."

"To hell with that." Regan got to her knees. Wobbled. Found what little balance she had. She stood up slowly, nearly tipping over several times.

"Regan, trust your instincts. You know if you can do it or not."

She couldn't do it. She knew that as plain as the nose on her face, but that meant nothing. She'd do it just to show him that you could do something impossible if you believed in yourself enough.

"Find something dead ahead to focus on. Don't look down."

A branch on a pine tree ahead of her had been sawn off some years ago. About fifteen feet off the ground, its stump kept her gaze level.

She began to walk.

Everything else faded away. Her focus tightened to the sawn-off branch stub, the log beneath her feet and Mason's quiet voice leading her across the distance to the other side.

She steadied as she went, finding a concentration she never knew she had. Now the end of the log was fifteen feet away. Ten feet. Five feet.

"You can do it."

Regan started, wavered, caught herself.

Ran the last few feet—

And pitched over the side.

"Regan!"

Her fall took less than a moment, but it was long enough for her to brace for the impact. An impact that didn't come.

Mason caught her in his arms and crushed her to his chest. "Regan. Are you okay?"

She blinked at him through suddenly-full eyes when she saw the love and concern in his face.

"I knew you would catch me." She reached up and

kissed him, crushing her bare breasts against his chest. Mason moaned against her as she turned in his arms.

"Let's go back to the Hall."

She pulled back. "Not until we see who wins this race. And by the way—you still have to do the balance beam." She wrenched out of his arms and darted away, laughing at Mason's disbelieving shouts behind her.

She stayed ahead of him until she reached the salmon ladder. Faced with this impossible obstacle, she didn't know what to do.

"Girls do twenty pull-ups," Mason called as he leaped past her, grabbed the bar on his salmon ladder, pulled up and pumped his legs to pop it up a rung.

Pull-ups? When was the last time she'd done pull-ups?

She got started, doing four quickly, but slowing down for five, six and seven. She had to pause to rest between each one until she reached ten, and then she thought she couldn't do anymore. She jumped down and paced in a circle, noticing only then that Mason had slowed down, too. Last time he had popped right up the ladder, one rung after another.

"What's wrong?"

"Pulled a muscle in my arm." He scrunched his face into an exaggeration of pain.

"Looks more like you're constipated."

Mason laughed and dropped from the salmon ladder. He looked surprised to find himself on his feet beneath it.

"Better start over, sailor!"

She gripped the pull-up bar again. Did two more. Three. Four. The spaces between pull ups got longer and longer. Five. Six. Seven.

Suddenly Mason began to pop up the ladder again. At her shout of frustration, he yelled down, "A miraculous recovery!"

She pulled up again for all she was worth. Eight. Nine.

Ten.

She leaped down and ran for the finish line, the thud behind her telling her Mason was done with his obstacle, too. There was no way she could beat him in a flat out sprint. This called for deviousness.

As his footsteps pounded up behind her, she leaped sideways, crashed into him and knocked them both to the ground.

"What the hell?"

Before he could catch his bearings, she shimmied beneath him, slipping her jean shorts and panties off right over her shoes. Suddenly naked, she popped up from under him and danced around, then dashed for the finish line.

"Wait—Regan!"

He came after her, caught her around the waist and they crashed to the ground again.

"Damn it. This isn't how you run an obstacle course," Mason protested. He'd fallen in such a way as to cushion the blow for her.

She smothered his protests in kisses. "But it's a lot more fun, isn't it?"

"You'd better not do this when my brothers get home."

She hopped off of him and but before she could made a break for the finish line, he was on his feet, pulling her into a searing hot kiss. Regan forgot the obstacle course momentarily. It had been a few days since they'd been together and her body wanted more. He fumbled with his belt, and she helped him undo it, then struggled with the button of his jeans. She pulled him along toward the finish line as she worked on it, unzipping his fly, reaching into his pants.

Taking hold of him.

She wrapped her free arm around his neck, kissed him and stroked him all at once, still retreating backward. She had to get to the finish line.

Mason kicked off his shoes, shucked off his jeans as they went and pulled them free of his legs, then lifted her right off her feet, wrapping her legs around his waist.

Regan let out a cry as he pressed against her core, forgetting everything but Mason. When he laid her down on the ground she welcomed his weight on top of her.

He gathered her close, kissing her mouth, her jaw, her throat, tracing his lips down to circle her breasts. Regan, coming alive beneath him, couldn't get enough. She wanted him closer. Wanted him inside of her.

When he pulled away she cried out in disappointment.

"Regan, honey." He let the moment draw out, his

gaze searching hers. "Will you marry me?"

"Yes!" She didn't have to think about it. Didn't care what their future brought. All she wanted was him. To be with him. He kissed her long and thoroughly, then lowered his face to rasp his cheek over the delicate skin of her breasts. The stubble of his beard chafed her, but she reveled in it, gasping with pleasure. When he took a nipple into his mouth, she arched back with a low, animal moan.

He laved her nipples to peaks, cupped and squeezed her full breasts and worshipped each of them in turn. When he sank lower, she writhed at the exquisite torture of his tongue exploring her sensitive folds.

"You need to cancel that doctor's appointment," he said, pulling away momentarily. "We'll start a family the old-fashioned way whenever you're ready."

"Right now," she gasped. "Mason, right now."

He stilled. "Are you sure?"

"Yes."

"But—"

"Mason!"

Her cry of frustration must have convinced him, because he surged up over her, nudged her thighs apart roughly with his own and found her hot, wet and ready for him. He positioned himself, pulled Regan close and surged inside her.

She cried out her pleasure and he did it again, his strong hard strokes quickly driving her to the brink of passion. "Mason—"

He got the message. He stroked into her again and again, laced his fingers with hers up over her head, exposing her to his view, and increased his pace, pulling out and thrusting in until she rocked with his movements, gasping and crying out. Mason pumped his body, his muscles gripping and releasing, and worked Regan over and over until she went right over the edge with another cry. Bucking and grunting his release too, he collapsed on top of her, fighting for breath.

When her heart rate had slowed and Regan came back to herself, she marveled at the man above her and how much she loved him.

Speaking of which.

She turned her head and spotted the white posts of the finish line just behind her. She untangled her fingers from Mason's, reached up to press her mouth to his, raised her arm up and over her shoulder and smacked her hand down on the dirt.

"I won!"

MASON HAD JUST gotten out of the shower when two trucks drove up the lane. Peering out of the tower bedroom curtains, he pulled on fresh clothes quickly and was downstairs before the truck doors opened and a handful of men and women spilled out.

"Mason?" the man in the lead called out to him. A tall cowboy with dark hair and blue eyes, he looked familiar and Mason searched his memory until he placed him.

"Noah Turner?"

"Got it on your first try." Noah came to shake his hand. "You remember Liam."

"Of course." He shook Liam's hand, too.

"And Stella and Maya."

Mason had known all four of the Turner siblings back in his school days. Emma Larson had driven the second truck and she came up to say hello. He wondered who the others were. The three men bore a resemblance to Noah and Liam, but he didn't recognize them.

"Nice of you to come to call. Let me round up Regan and we'll make you all some lunch."

"This isn't a social call, Mason."

Damn. His good mood began to fade. Were they here to collect another debt? Did Noah think he needed to bring a posse?

"We're here to work," one of the men he didn't know said. "Where do we start?"

His expression must have conveyed his confusion. Emma stepped forward. "Allen James spread the word around that you and Regan could use some help out here. Regan mentioned something similar the night she helped me with my loan paperwork, so I decided it was my turn to lend a hand. The rest of the gang decided to tag along."

"These troublemakers are my cousins—Eli, Brody and Alex Turner," Noah put in. "They moved to town to help us out last year, after my father had a stroke. Now we're working the Flying W together.

Mason quickly shook hands with all of them, but he felt like he couldn't keep up. "You're here to help? You sure my uncle Zeke doesn't owe you money?"

Noah chuckled. "Heard about that, too. Don't worry—I'm too cheap to lend money to anyone. And even if I had, I'd still come to help you. I know you won't hit me up for cash."

"Don't be too sure." Mason couldn't keep the sour note out of his voice. "You haven't seen the state of the place."

The women went inside to find Regan, while the men headed out to the pasture with the unfinished fence. In no time at all, they'd completed that job and had moved on to another pasture, working together with the ease of long acquaintances, until Mason felt almost redundant. He missed Regan's cheerful presence working beside him—and their games—but he was more grateful than he could say to have the extra hands.

The Turners were all strong men who'd been working on ranches for years, so the job went smoothly. Soon after lunch—a picnic prepared by the women and brought out to them to eat on a checkered tablecloth—they caught up to where Mason had wanted to be.

"You must have things to do back at your place," he said to the others. He didn't know how he'd accomplish the rest with a single set of hands, but he didn't want to impose on friends.

"I'd say there's more to do here." Noah cocked his hat back and rubbed his wrist over his forehead. The day was warmer than it had been.

"There's a lot more," Mason admitted.

"You got a list or is it in your head?" Liam asked.

Mason pulled the rumpled timeline from the front seat of his truck and showed them. Liam, tall and dark like his brother, about twenty-six years old to Noah's twenty-eight, looked it over. "I reckon we could give you a few hours a day for the next week or so and get it all done."

"We can put the word out, too," Noah said. "There are lots of people who remember your family, Mason. They'll want to help all they can. You've got your plan. It'll just be a matter of delegating jobs when people show up."

Mason nodded. Just what he'd hoped for when he'd first arrived in town. "I appreciate what you're doing."

"What's next?" Alex asked, flipping a hammer in his hand. The Colorado Turners bore a distinct family resemblance to Noah and Liam—strong, broad-shouldered, clear-eyed.

"We've got a couple more pastures to do. Then we need to fix the roof of the Hall."

Five pairs of eyes turned toward the tall structure. Noah scratched his head. "No offense, but I'm not looking forward to that."

REGAN CAME TO the front hall when she heard voices calling her name and found three women looking for her. She recognized Emma Larson, but the other two were strangers.

"Hi, Regan. I brought you some company," Emma said. She made the introductions, telling Regan that Stella and Maya lived on the Flying W ranch with their brothers and cousins, who had come to help Mason with the rest of the fencing.

Regan led them all out to the back porch and served them lemonade. "I was just about to make lunch."

"Let the men work a bit and then we'll help you. We can have a picnic," Emma suggested. "I brought some goodies along, too. I hoped you'd taste-test them." She patted the basket she carried. She seemed excited and before Regan could ask if she'd had any news, she burst out, "I got my loan! I know your help made all the difference. I'm going to tell everyone about what you did. You'll be swimming in customers for your consulting services."

"That's wonderful!" Regan hugged her. "I'm so happy for you. When will the purchase go through?"

"Next month. I can't wait. I'm finally going to have my own bakery."

"Will you sell cupcakes?" Stella Turner was a vivacious brunette with laughing hazel eyes.

"Of course. I'll sell everything I can think of."

Stella peered down the track where the men had disappeared to the far pastures. "Normally I'd be out there with the men," she confided to Regan. "I work the ranch with my brothers and cousins. Live for riding horses and all that. But I wanted to meet you first. Allen James thought you were just the ticket for Mason. I can see what he means."

Maya was quieter, but no less welcoming. Twenty-four, with light brown hair and blue eyes, she seemed a little dreamy. Regan wondered if a man was the subject of those dreams, but there was no ring on Maya's finger and she didn't feel she knew the young woman well enough to ask.

"How are you adjusting to ranch life?" Stella didn't hide her curiosity. "Emma says you're a city girl."

"That's right. At first it was a bit of a shock, but I think I'll get used to it okay. I love the view and the quiet. I like working with Mason, too," Regan said.

"Are you two getting married?" Maya asked shyly.

Regan smiled. "Yes." The thought made her tingle down to her toes.

"It takes courage to move to a new place and start over." Emma made a face. "I'm so glad to be coming home. Are you settling in okay? You haven't been much to town."

"We haven't had time. It's been a little lonely," Regan admitted, "but I was lonely in New York, too. My two best friends had moved away." She hadn't spoken to either of them in weeks now. She'd hesitated to call and tell them what she'd been doing. Traveling to Montana with a man she'd just met? They'd both be on planes to fetch her home first thing.

"Well, now you have three friends. I'm glad you've moved here. Chance Creek can use some new blood now and then."

Regan returned Emma's smile. The woman was glowing with happiness over getting her loan, and she felt gratified she'd played a small part in helping her secure it. Would there be enough consulting work in Chance Creek to make money? She didn't know, but if the last few weeks had been any indication, there was plenty of work here on the ranch for her to do. Maybe consulting could be a part-time gig. She liked Emma, Stella and Maya. They were practical women with a fun-loving streak. The kind of friends she liked the best. She was beginning to think that life on the ranch would be far more active and interesting than life in the city had ever been.

"Do you have plans for fixing up the Hall?" Emma asked.

Regan snapped back to the present. Did she ever. "Want a tour?"

The women eagerly got to their feet. As Regan led them around the first floor, she discussed all the ideas she had so far. "I told Mason to get his mother to send us pictures of the way it used to be furnished so I can try to replicate it."

Maya gasped. "I know where to start. Redder's Auction House. That's where Zeke brought all the things he wanted to sell."

Stella turned on her. "How on earth do you know that?"

"Deal told me. My boyfriend," she explained to Regan. "Art Redder is his uncle and he works for him sometimes, clearing out houses and loading up trucks. Deal told me once that Zeke Hall kept bringing things in one at a time to Art and it was driving Art crazy. He likes to buy big lots all at once. That's how he makes his money."

"Do you think Mr. Redder would remember who he sold them to?"

"He's bound to. He keeps records of everything." When Stella raised an eyebrow Maya shrugged. "That's what Deal says."

"If he's right it'll be the first helpful thing Deal's ever done in his life."

Regan decided to steer the conversation away from this apparently controversial subject. Maya had pressed her lips together in a thin line and her face was turning pink. "Can you take me to the auction house some time?"

"I'd be glad to."

"How about we make the men some lunch."

CHAPTER SIXTEEN

TWO WEEKS LATER, Mason surveyed the ranch with satisfaction. The pastures were ready for cattle, the barn and stables were in good repair. Even the Hall's exterior looked better than it previously had. Alex had turned out to be the best with heights, and he'd joined Mason on the roof to replace its missing shingles. The rest of the men had measured up the broken windows and installed their replacements.

Regan had made headway on the Hall's interior, with help from the Turner women. She'd painted most of the first floor, had dug layers of grime out of the corners and crevices of the old house, and spruced up everything she could. They had a long way to go, but they'd made a good start.

Today Mason's task was to sand all the hardwood floors with a large electric sander he'd rented for the day. Then he'd need to get busy staining and sealing them with polyurethane. They'd set their wedding for the third week in June, and while the Hall would remain a work in progress, there was no reason they couldn't have the floors done by then.

Regan was gone for the day with her new friend, Maya Turner, but he didn't mind the solitude. In fact, he felt more content than he had in a long time. None of his brothers could report progress on the marriage front, but he had faith it would all turn out. Meanwhile, he enjoyed the hard physical work and the sense of accomplishment he felt at the end of each day.

His favorite time was when he and Regan sat on the back porch and watched the sunset, drinking a beer together before heading up to bed. He had the feeling he'd be just as happy to sit with her there forty years in the future as he was right now. Each time he saw his diamond engagement ring on her finger, he felt a surge of satisfaction. It wasn't the fanciest ring, but Regan hadn't seemed to mind when he slid it on her finger a few days after they'd gotten engaged at the finish line of the Course. These days when he looked at her he saw the same happiness shining back at him in her eyes as he felt in his heart.

Mason had just turned off the loud sander to take a break when the front door banged open and Regan shouted to him.

"Come here! I've got your wedding present."

"Isn't it a little early for that?" He made his way to the front hall where she stuck her head in the door, her thick auburn hair caught up in a French braid.

"Engagement present then. Come look!"

He followed her out the door in time to see two men in coveralls with Redder's Auctions blazoned on the back lifting a large, solid walnut dining room table out of the back of a delivery truck. He saw chairs stacked inside the truck, too.

He took the stairs down two at a time to inspect the furniture more closely. "That's our table. Where'd you find it?"

"Maya helped me," Regan said, joining him. "She introduced me to Art Redder and he helped me track down some of the things Zeke sold. I found a display cabinet and a couple of end tables from the living room, a painting of the ranch that Redder says used to hang in the front hall, and the cast-iron bunk beds from the bunkhouse."

Mason chuckled. "I hope you didn't pay too much for those."

She shook her head. "I got those back for free. They didn't fit where they were supposed to go and they're so heavy the man who bought them said he kept putting off hauling them away. He was glad to see them go."

"The table and chairs were the most important." He ran a hand over its broad, scarred surface. "My family made a lot of memories around this table."

"I can't wait to make some of our own."

Mason pitched in and helped carry the overlong table into the formal Hall dining room.

He couldn't wait either.

CHAPTER SEVENTEEN

NOW TWO OF the handsome military heroes from the Wife Wanted ad had come to life. Austin arrived at the ranch late in the afternoon on the Thursday before Regan's wedding to Mason. Mason had been waiting for his brother's arrival for weeks. Austin was home for good now that all his obligations to the Army were fulfilled.

The last few weeks had been so busy Regan couldn't believe how fast the time had gone. She'd cancelled her insemination appointment right after she accepted Mason's proposal, and had taken a quick trip back to New York a week later to box up her things and return the key to her apartment. Since then she'd worked as hard and as fast as she could to get the Hall into shape.

She'd gotten help from Emma, Stella and Maya to plan a small family wedding to be held on the wide back lawn. If the weather had turned rainy, they would have moved everything inside the house, but their luck held and the weekend ahead of them was forecasted to be uniformly sunny and warm.

Stella and Maya knew everyone in town and helped her locate a caterer and party rental company. Emma insisted on making her cake and Regan spent a fun afternoon with her pouring over the possibilities and tasting several varieties of cake and frosting. All three of them had accompanied her to pick a dress out at Ellie's Bridals.

In the end she chose one with a sleeveless boned corset and a sweeping skirt. As she stood on the pedestal to model it to the others, she felt like she'd stepped into a fairy-tale. She'd never worn anything so beautiful.

"There, what do you think?" Ellie, the owner of the store, asked, fluffing out the full skirt and stepping back to survey her handiwork.

"It's gorgeous. And your hair is to die for!" Emma fingered her own blonde ponytail. "You look like a princess."

"She's got such a tiny waist!" Maya stood with hands on hips, evaluating her.

"That's the one. It's got to be," Stella said. All of them nodded.

Regan's heart had swelled. All of her dreams were coming true. She wasn't going to be alone for the rest of her life. She wouldn't have to be a single mother trying to do everything herself. She'd have a husband, a family—a home. She almost couldn't believe it.

While her sister would be her maid of honor, Emma, Stella and Maya had all agreed to be her bridesmaids, since it turned out to be too difficult for either of her old best friends to fly out to Montana for the wedding. Austin was to be Mason's best man and his other two brothers would stand up with him as well. Her parents and Mason's mother were flying in on Friday evening. Zane and Colt would arrive earlier that day. Saturday was the wedding. Every time Regan thought of it she had to take deep breaths.

She and Mason came out to greet Austin as soon as he drove up in his rental truck. He'd flown into the Chance Creek Regional Airport, but told them he preferred to drive himself home. Regan held back while the brothers executed a semi-awkward man-hug, but then stepped forward to shake Austin's hand.

He was as tall and broad as Mason, with intelligent eyes and an intensity she remembered Mason possessing when she first met him. Maybe that was from his recent stint in a conflict zone. Austin shook her hand, then tugged her in for a hug. "You managed to trick this beauty into marrying you?" he said over his shoulder to Mason. "You're a lucky son-of-a-gun!" He released Regan and she stumbled back, overwhelmed and embarrassed. "God, it's good to be home," Austin went on. "I can't believe the Hall is home again."

"I know what you mean." Mason grabbed Austin's bags and led the way inside.

"I've never seen the place so empty of cattle before. It's not right."

"We'll start looking for horses as soon as I'm back from my honeymoon and soon enough the place will be crawling with critters," Mason assured him.

"It's nice in here. You painted. The floors look great, too." Austin looked around the first floor appreciatively. "A lot of the furniture is still missing, though."

"Regan's been tracking it down piece by piece." He led Austin into the dining room and showed him the table and the chandelier she'd located soon afterward. "She found this at least. And we bought you a new bed. Now that you're here you can help us with the rest."

Austin nodded. "I didn't think Zeke had it in him to strip the ranch like this."

"Me, either. But it's not too far gone. We'll fix it up again."

Regan trailed the brothers as Mason showed Austin the rest of the repairs they'd made around the place. They walked the length of the closest pasture down to the banks of Chance Creek, talking all the way about their respective deployments and other family gossip.

"Got a girlfriend?" Mason asked his brother at one point.

"Maybe." Austin smiled but didn't elaborate. "How about the Course?" He turned toward the woods at the edge of the large lawn. "Is it still there?"

"Still there. We've run it a couple of times."

"Oh, yeah? Bet I can beat you now. Never could catch you when we were kids."

"Bet you still can't."

A moment later the two men had taken off, racing like boys across the grass toward the start of the obstacle course. Regan laughed, but quickly jogged after them. She didn't want to miss this.

"Regan, call the start." Mason and his brother were crouched and ready at the starting line, taut with anticipation for the race.

"On your mark. Get set. Go!"

She stepped back as both men leaped toward the monkey bars. Across them in seconds, they were off, pounding through the woods toward the vertical wall. Regan sprang forward in time to see both men hit it at a dead run, their fingers gripping the top of the wall, their feet kicking against it for purchase until they hauled themselves up and over and disappeared.

Regan ran forward to try to see more of the race, but they moved so fast she could barely keep up. She had a glimpse of them pounding through the tire course on the ground, another of them army crawling under the lengths of barbed wire. She raced along the central path as they hit the next few obstacles, then bit her lip as Austin and Mason charged up the incline logs to the balance beams. Surely one of them would break his neck.

They set off across the horizontal logs at a dead run. Regan clapped a hand to her mouth. When they both made it to the far end she finally let go of the breath she'd been holding.

They raced to the vertical salmon ladders and swung and grunted their way up to the top. Regan cut back to meet the men at the finish line while they completed the other obstacles. When she reached the edge of the forest, Mason and Austin had just begun the final dash.

She couldn't tell who was ahead from here. They looked neck and neck, running so fast their feet ate up the ground. These weren't the kind of showy body builders she'd seen in fitness centers in New York City. These were men who used their bodies as weapons. Men who defended their country. Men who would fight to the death.

She held her breath as the two men raced right past. If one of them had won, Regan couldn't tell.

"I won!" Austin crowed, coming to a stop, his shoulders heaving as he bent over and braced his hands against his thighs, winded.

"Are you kidding? I won," Mason countered, walking in a small circle and breathing hard, too.

"It was a tie," Regan said definitively. "Now go on home and wash up for supper." She chuckled at their equally disgruntled expressions.

CHAPTER EIGHTEEN

THAT NIGHT, MASON settled down to sleep with Regan. "Ready for a full house?" He kissed her shoulder, drawing her close under the covers. She'd given up on nightclothes since, as she put it, he kept taking them off of her as fast as she could put anything on.

"I think so."

"Nervous?"

"A little. I keep thinking there's something I've forgotten."

"I know exactly what you forgot."

"What?" She half sat up, but he drew her down again.

"To make love to me."

"Mason." But she giggled as he kissed her neck and then trailed his lips down to her breasts. "I'm serious."

He sighed. "Do you have a dress?"

"Of course!"

"Shoes?"

"Yes."

"Food?"

"Uh-huh."

"Alcohol?"

"That goes without saying." She tweaked his nose.

"And I know you've got a preacher, since I'm the one who lined that up, so we're all set. Quit worrying!" He tugged her close and kissed her before she could think of anything else to say. He didn't mean to be distracted from accomplishing this mission: making sweet love to her as many times as she let him.

He allowed his hands to slide over her body, luxuriating in every sweet curve of it. He was already hard and ready to go—his body knew just what to expect when they went to bed—but he also knew they had time and he meant to make the most of it. The next few days would be busy ones and their honeymoon would be all too short before it was back to the grueling work schedule they'd kept up since they'd arrived home.

He rolled over onto his back and pulled Regan up on top of him. She straddled him happily and he sighed when he felt her silky softness pressed up against him. It would be so easy to shift his hips and push inside her. She was as ready as he was for that, but he wanted to take this slow and enjoy every minute of it.

She rocked her hips lightly and he groaned. "You look good up there," he said, cupping her breasts. She always looked good.

She smiled. "You make me feel beautiful when you look at me like that."

"You are beautiful." He stroked one of her breasts

lightly, then the other, then lifted them one at a time to his mouth. Regan sighed and leaned forward to make them more accessible. He took his time, used his tongue and teeth to caress her until she moaned.

In time Mason slid his hands down her back, over her ass and up again, each time settling her a little closer until he could tell she was as desperate as he was for him to slide inside.

Still, they spun things out, taking time to kiss hungrily, nip at each other's skin and stroke each other until Mason hummed with longing for more.

But when she pulled away from him, slid down between his legs and took him into her mouth, he groaned and lay back, allowing her to have her way with him. She took him in, then slid him out, her mouth caressing the length of him. She stroked her hands over his powerful thighs, pulling him in deeper until it strained his very ability to maintain control. When he tangled his fingers into her hair and moved with her, she slid her hands under his ass and pulled him closer.

"Regan." His voice was husky. After a few moments, he reached down and tugged her back up on top of him. "I can't wait." She pushed up with her knees and settled back down on top of him, pushing him slowly inside.

Mason nearly lost it right then. She felt so good—hot, wet, inviting him to stroke in and fill her. With his hands gripping her hips, he pulled out and surged in again. Holding back took every ounce of willpower he'd ever had, but he was damned if he would cut this short. He meant to make love to her all night.

Soon they found their tempo, the friction between them driving them to ever higher heights. Regan rode his thrusts with the abandon of full trust, letting him plunge in and out and take everything he needed. He watched the rise and fall of her breasts and his gaze on her body seemed to make her more wanton. She arched her back, met his thrusts and when her release came she cried out with the joy of it. Mason joined her, grunting as he bucked against her, fingers digging into her hips, splayed over her ass. He let himself go and she teased him along into a release that left him limp with utter exhaustion.

She collapsed on top him and he circled her with his arms, content to stay like this for the rest of their lives.

REGAN WAS GLAD she'd had a day to get used to Austin before Zane came home. If she'd met them together she would have struggled to tell one from the other. With their dark hair and piercing hazel eyes, they were almost as handsome as their older brother.

Almost, but not quite. Zane was quicker to laugh than Austin, who could be cheerful one minute and dead serious the next. She thought of Austin as being the older twin although Zane informed her he'd come into the world five whole minutes before Austin made his appearance.

No sooner had Zane arrived and they'd settled him in a bedroom at the Hall, then they were back at the airport picking up Colt. He was blond, with a nervous energy and quick wit that told her he'd be a handful. In a quiet moment after they returned home, Mason confirmed this. "Whatever Austin, Zane and I choose to do, Colt picks the opposite path. I can't believe the Air Force lets him near their planes—expensive ones!"

"Are there any other kind?"

Later, the brothers convened on the back porch, beers in hand, to catch up. Regan's family and other guests would arrive the following day, so this was the first and last chance for the brothers to be alone together. Regan tried to busy herself inside and give them some privacy, but Mason insisted she join them, too. "You're family now."

As they filled each other in on the news, Regan found herself smiling. She liked these rough and tumble brothers with their gallant manners towards women and winner-take-all attitude toward the rest of mankind.

"You found yourself a hell of a woman, there," Zane spoke up. He raised his bottle. "To Regan. May we all be so lucky!"

The others raised their beers and toasted her.

Colt emptied his drink and set it down. "You never told us how you got Mason to change his mind." When Mason raised an eyebrow he went on. "You said you had a few tricks up your sleeve to convince him to stay here and fix up the Hall."

Regan blushed at the memory of her naked romp through the obstacle course, while Mason laughed out loud. "Should we keep that one a secret, honey?" he nudged her foot with his.

"You'd better." But for one moment she wished all their guests would leave so they could do it all over again.

CHAPTER NINETEEN

"ONE DOWN, THREE to go," Aunt Heloise announced when she arrived the morning of the wedding, driven by Allen James. Mason was glad his new in-laws weren't in earshot. Regan might understand the circumstances of the Wife Wanted ad, but he doubted her parents—a friendly down-to-earth couple who'd taken to Mason at first sight—would.

"We're working on it," Austin assured her. "We'll get 'er done."

"Even you?" Heloise jabbed a finger in Colt's bicep. "I seem to remember you were always the ornery one."

"I guess I'll have to find an ornery way to get married then." He flashed her a wolfish grin.

"See that you do. I love all my grand-nephews equally, but I'm not happy about the idea of leaving the Hall to Darren. He'd probably just undo all the progress you made. Are you working on that heir?" she added, pinning Mason with a sharp gaze.

"It's got my full attention, believe me."

"Humph. Better get a move on. When does this

shindig get started?"

"Soon." He guided her to a seat near a table in the kitchen where Emma Larson was touching up the wedding cake she'd made.

"Oh, that's beautiful, dear," Heloise was saying when Mason returned to his brothers.

"Nervous?" Zane asked.

"A little." A lot, actually. He hadn't felt this shaky since he'd been caught in a firefight back in Afghanistan.

"You'll do fine. I can't believe how much you and Regan managed to do with the ranch already." Austin nudged him. "Dad would be proud."

Mason straightened his shoulders. He did think his father would be proud of him—not for fixing the ranch up so much as for finding a woman to share his life with and dedicating himself to being the best husband he could to her. His dad had always put his family ahead of everything else.

"Think Regan's got a friend?" Colt asked.

"I'm sure she does. Want me to ask her to find you a wife?"

"Who's finding who a wife?" Mason's mom swooped down upon them and gave them each a kiss on the cheek. "Look at my boys. All of you are so handsome. Any woman would be lucky to have you."

"You're a little biased, don't you think?" But Austin was grinning as widely as any of them.

"I'm allowed to be biased. I'm your mother. And you've picked out a lovely wife, Mason. I just had a good long chat with Regan. The two of you will make a fine couple."

"As good as you and dad?"

Her smile trembled as tears shone in her eyes. "I'd say better, but I don't think that's possible."

Mason spotted Regan consulting with Emma over the cake and his heartbeat sped up. Would she ever stop having that effect on him? He doubted it.

His mother followed his gaze. "You'll do just fine."

AS REGAN'S FATHER walked her down the aisle, the man at the end of it held her attention—and her heart—like no one else had ever done. She loved everything about Mason, from his strength and confidence, to his deeply caring soul. She'd seen him angry and she'd seen him loving and she knew he was the man she wanted always by her side.

She said her vows with her heart pounding and listened to his careful replies, hardly believing she was the one this handsome man had picked for his bride. But when the minister pronounced them man and wife and Mason bent to kiss her, his mouth on hers was so familiar, and so right, that she knew without a doubt that it was all true.

The rest of the day passed in a blur of family, friends, toasts, a first dance and cutting the cake. When darkness fell, they climbed into a classic limousine and were whisked away to a beautiful lodge in the mountains not too far away. With the Hall and ranch needing so much work, they'd decided time together was what they wanted more than an exotic vacation. That would have to wait for another year. For now a bed—and privacy—was what they wanted most.

As Mason undressed her, inch by inch, Regan gloried in the knowledge they would never be apart again. It didn't matter how they'd come together. It was being together that counted, and they were experts at that.

Still, when she stepped out of her dress, Mason reached for her with a hunger that was all too evident in his eyes. She knew her bustier and garters excited him. Knew too he'd have them off her in no time. As the first strap snapped between his fingers she shut her eyes and laughed.

"What?"

"Nothing." She smiled at him, knowing the depth of her love for him must be obvious in her expression.

"This?" He snapped another strap, then ripped the two sides of the bustier apart. "No matter what you wear you can't hide from me," he mock-growled.

"I guess not." She allowed him to lay her back on the bed, sighed as he peeled the garment off of her. "But you haven't even let me give you your wedding present yet."

"I thought you were my wedding present."

"No. This is." She reached into the bag she'd placed near the bed for just this moment and pulled out a plastic test wand. "We're pregnant."

Mason stilled beside her. "Are you sure?"

"Here's the proof." She waved it at him.

He took it from her. Read the result. Tossed it over his shoulder and scooped her into his arms. "That's the best gift you could ever give me."

"Because it means you get to keep the ranch?"

He cupped her face between his hands. "Because it means you love me enough to share something so precious with me." He kissed her soundly. "You won't regret this, you know. Being my wife. Letting me love you for the rest of your life."

No, she knew she wouldn't regret it. Naked in Mason's bed, filled by him, loved by him.

That's where she belonged.

THE END

The Heroes of Chance Creek series continues with The Soldier's E-Mail Order Bride.

Read on for an excerpt of Volume 1 of **The Cowboys of Chance Creek** series – *The Cowboy's E-Mail Order Bride*. Please note that this novel is not part of the Heroes of Chance Creek series; it is the first in the earlier series, The Cowboys of Chance Creek.

Other Titles by Cora Seton:

The Heroes of Chance Creek:

The Soldier's E-Mail Order Bride (Volume 2)
The Marine's E-Mail Order Bride (Volume 3)
The Airman's E-Mail Order Bride (Volume 4)

The Cowboys of Chance Creek:

The Cowboy's E-mail Order Bride (Volume 1)
The Cowboy Wins a Bride (Volume 2)
The Cowboy Imports a Bride (Volume 3)
The Cowgirl Ropes a Billionaire (Volume 4)
The Sheriff Catches a Bride (Volume 5)
The Cowboy Lassos a Bride (Volume 6)
The Cowboy Rescues a Bride (Volume 7)
The Cowboy Earns a Bride (Volume 8)

Chapter One

"YOU DID WHAT?" Ethan Cruz turned his back on the slate and glass entrance to Chance Creek, Montana's Regional Airport, and jiggled the door handle of Rob Matheson's battered red Chevy truck. Locked. It figured—Rob had to know he'd want to turn tail and head back to town the minute he found out what his friends had done. "Open the damned door, Rob."

"Not a chance. You've got to come in—we're picking up your bride."

"I don't have a bride and no one getting off that plane concerns me. You've had your fun, now open up the door or I'm grabbing a taxi." He faced his friends. Rob, who'd lived on the ranch next door to his their entire lives. Cab Johnson, county sheriff, who was far too level-headed to be part of this mess. And Jamie Lassiter, the best horse trainer west of the Mississippi as long as you could pry him away from the ladies. The four of them had gone to school together, played football together, and spent more Saturday nights at the bar than he could count. How many times had he gotten them out of trouble, drove them home when they'd had one beer to many, listened to them bellyache about their girlfriends or lack thereof when all he really wanted to do was knock back a cold one and play a game of pool? What the hell had he ever done to deserve this?

Unfortunately, he knew exactly what he'd done. He'd played a spectacularly brilliant prank a month or so ago on Rob—a prank that still had the town buzzing—and Rob concocted this nightmare as payback. Rob got him drunk one night and egged him on about his ex-fiancee until he spilled his guts about how much it still bothered him that Lacey Taylor had given him the boot in favor of that rich sonofabitch Carl Whitfield. The name made him want to spit. Dressed like a cowboy when everyone knew he couldn't ride to save his life.

Lacey bailed on him just as life had delivered a walloping one-two punch. First his parents died in a car accident. Then he discovered the ranch was mortgaged to the hilt. As soon as Lacey learned there would be some hard times ahead, she took off like a runaway horse. Didn't even have the decency to break up with him face to face. Before he knew it Carl was flying Lacey all over creation in his private plane. Las Vegas. San Francisco. Houston. He never had a chance to get her back.

He should have kept his thoughts bottled up where

they belonged—would have kept them bottled up if Rob hadn't kept putting those shots into his hand—but no, after he got done swearing and railing at Lacey's bad taste in men, he apparently decided to lecture his friends on the merits of a real woman. The kind of woman a cowboy should marry.

And Rob—good ol' Rob—captured the whole thing with his cell phone.

When he showed it to him the following day, Ethan made short work of the asinine gadget, but it was too late. Rob had already emailed the video to Cab and Jamie, and the three of them spent the next several days making his life damn miserable over it.

If only they'd left it there.

The other two would have, but Rob was still sore about that old practical joke, so he took things even further. He decided there must be a woman out there somewhere who met all of the requirements Ethan expounded on during his drunken rant. To find her, he did what any rational man would do. He edited Ethan's rant into a video advertisement for a damned mail order bride.

And posted it on YouTube.

Rob showed him the video on the ride over to the airport. There he was for all the world to see, sounding like a jack-ass—hell, looking like one, too. Rob's fancy editing made his rant sound like a proposition. "What I want," he heard himself say, "is a traditional bride. A bride for a cowboy. 18—25 years old, willing to work hard, beautiful, quiet, sweet, good cook, ready for children. I'm willing to give her a trial. One month'll tell me all I need to know." Then the image cut out to a screen full of text, telling women how to submit their video applications.

Unbelievable. This was low—real low—even for Rob.

Ready for children?

"You all are cracked in the head. I'm not going in there."

"Come on, Ethan," Cab said. The big man stood with his legs spread, his arms folded over his barrel chest, ready to stop him if he tried to run. "The girl's come all the way from New York. You're not even going to say hello? What kind of a fiance are you?"

He clenched his fists. "No kind at all. And there isn't any girl in there. You know it. I know it. So stop wasting my time. There isn't any girl dumb enough to answer something like that!"

The other men exchanged a look.

"Actually," Jamie said, leaning against the Chevy and rubbing the stubble on his chin with the back of his hand. "We got nearly 200 answers to that video. Took us hours to get through them all." He grinned. "Who can resist a cowboy, right?"

As far as Ethan was concerned, plenty of women could. Lacey certainly had resisted him. Hence his bachelor status. "So you picked the ugliest, dumbest girl and tricked her into buying a plane ticket. Terrific."

Rob looked pained. "No, we found one that's both hot and smart. And we chipped in and bought the ticket—round trip, because we figured you wouldn't know a good thing when it kicked you in the butt, so we'd have to send her back. Have a little faith in your friends. You think we'd steer you wrong?"

Hell, yes. Ethan took a deep breath and squared his shoulders. The guys wouldn't admit they were joking until he'd gone into the airport and hung around the gate looking foolish for a suitable amount of time. And if they were stupid enough to actually fly a girl out here, he couldn't trust them to put her back on a plane home. So now instead of finishing his chores before supper, he'd lose the rest of the afternoon sorting out this mess.

"Fine. Let's get this over with," he said, striding toward the front door. Inside, he didn't bother to look at the television screen which showed incoming and outgoing flights. Chance Creek Regional had all of four gates. He'd just follow the hall as far as homeland security allowed him and wait until some lost soul deplaned.

"Look—it's on time." Rob grabbed his arm and tried to hurry him along. Ethan dug in the heels of his well worn boots and proceeded at his own pace.

Jamie pulled a cardboard sign out from under his jacket and flashed it at Ethan before holding it up above his head. It read, Autumn Leeds. Jamie shrugged at Ethan's expression. "I know—the name's brutal."

"Want to see her?" Cab pulled out a gadget and handed it over. Ethan held it gingerly. The laptop he bought on the advice of his accountant still sat untouched in his tiny office back at the ranch. He hated these miniature things that ran on swoops and swipes and taps on buttons that weren't really there. Cab reached over and pressed something and it came to life, showing a pretty young woman in a cotton dress in a kitchen preparing what appeared to be a pot roast.

"Hi, I'm Autumn," she said, looking straight at him. "Autumn Leeds. As you can see, I love cooking…"

Rob whooped and pointed. "Look—there she is! I told you she'd come!"

Ethan raised his gaze from the gadget to see the woman herself walking toward them down the carpeted hall. Long black hair, startling blue eyes, porcelain-white skin, she was thin and haunted and luminous all at the same time. She, too, held a cell phone and seemed to be consulting it, her gaze glancing down then sweeping the crowd. As their eyes met, hers widened with recognition. He groaned inwardly when he realized this pretty woman had probably watched Rob's stupid video multiple times. She might be looking at his picture now.

As the crowd of passengers and relatives split around their party, she walked straight up to them and held out her hand. "Ethan Cruz?" Her voice was low and husky, her fingers cool and her handshake firm. He found himself wanting to linger over it. Instead he nodded. "I'm Autumn Leeds. Your bride."

AUTUMN HAD NEVER BEEN more terrified in her life. In her short career as a columnist for CityPretty Magazine, she'd interviewed models, society women, CEO's and politicians, but all of them were urbanites, and she'd never had to leave New York to get the job done. As soon as her plane departed LaGuardia she knew she'd made a mistake. As the city skyline fell away and the countryside below her emptied into farmland, she clutched the arms of her seat as if she was heading for the moon rather than Montana. Now, hours later, she felt off-kilter and fuzzy, and the four men before her looked like extras in a Western flick. Large, muscled, rough men who all exuded a distinct odor of sweat she realized probably came from an honest afternoon's work. Entirely out of her comfort zone, she wondered for the millionth time if she'd done the right thing. It's the only way to get my contract renewed, she reminded herself. She had to write a story different from all the other articles in CityPretty. In these tough economic times, the magazine was downsizing—again. If she didn't want to find herself out on the street, she had to produce—fast.

And what better story to write than the tale of a Montana cowboy using YouTube to search for an email-order bride?

Ethan Cruz looked back at her, seemingly at a loss for words. Well, that was to be expected with a cowboy, right? The ones in movies said about one word every ten minutes or so. That's why his video said she needed to be quiet. Well, she could be quiet. She didn't trust herself to speak, anyway.

She'd never been so near a cowboy before. Her

best friend, Becka, helped shoot her video response, and they'd spent a hilarious day creating a pseudo-Autumn guaranteed to warm the cockles of a cowboy's heart. Together, they'd decided to pitch her as desperate to escape the dirty city and unleash her inner farm wife on Ethan's Montana ranch. They hinted she loved gardening, canning, and all the domestic arts. They played up both her toughness (she played first base in high school baseball) and her femininity (she loved quilting—*what an outright lie*). She had six costume changes in the three minute video.

Over her vehement protests, Becka forced her to end the video with a close-up of her face while she uttered the words, "I often fall asleep imagining the family I'll someday have." Autumn's cheeks warmed as she recalled the depth of the deception. She wasn't a country girl pining to be a wife; she was a career girl who didn't intend to have kids for at least another decade. Right?

Of course.

Except somehow, when she watched the final video, the life the false Autumn said she wanted sounded far more compelling than the life the real Autumn lived. Especially the part about wanting a family.

It wasn't that she didn't want a career. She just wanted a different one—a different life. She hated how hectic and shallow everything seemed now. She remembered her childhood, back when she had two parents—a successful investment banker father and a stay-at-home mother who made the best cookies in

New York City. Back then, her mom, Teresa, loved to take Autumn and her sister, Lily, to visit museums, see movies and plays, walk in Central Park and shop in the ethnic groceries that surrounded their home. On Sundays, they cooked fabulous feasts together and her mother's laugh rang out loud and often. Friends and relatives stopped by to eat and talk, and Autumn played with the other children while the grownups clustered around the kitchen table. All that changed when she turned nine and her father left them for a travel agent. Her parents' divorce was horrible. The fight wasn't over custody; her father was all too eager to leave child-rearing to her mother while he toured Brazil with his new wife. The fight was over money—over the bulk of the savings her father had transferred to offshore accounts in the weeks before the breakup, and refused to return.

Broke, single and humiliated, her mother took up the threads of the life she'd put aside to marry and raise a family. A graduate of an elite liberal arts college, with several years of medical school already under her belt, she moved them into a tiny apartment on the edge of a barely-decent neighborhood and returned to her studies. Those were lean, lonely years when everyone had to pitch in. Autumn's older sister watched over her after school, and Teresa expected them to take on any and all chores they could possibly handle. As Autumn grew, she took over the cooking and shopping and finally the family's accounts. Teresa had no time for cultural excursions, let alone entertaining friends, but by the time Autumn was ready to go to college herself, she ran a successful OB-GYN practice that catered to wealthy women who'd left childbearing until the last possible moment, and she didn't even have to take out a loan to fund her education.

Determined her daughters would never face the same challenges she had, Teresa raised them with three guiding precepts:

Every woman must be self-supporting.

Marriage is a trap set by men for women.

Parenthood must be postponed until one reaches the pinnacle of her career.

Autumn's sister, Lily, was a shining example of this guide to life. She was single, ran her own physical therapy clinic, and didn't plan to marry or have children any time soon. Next to her, Autumn felt like a black sheep. She couldn't seem to accept work was all there was to life. Couldn't forget the joy of laying a table for a host of guests. She still missed those happy, crowded Sunday afternoons so much it hurt her to think about them.

She forced her thoughts back to the present. The man before her was ten times more handsome than he was in his video, and that was saying a lot. Dark hair, blue eyes, a chiseled jaw with just a trace of manly stubble. His shoulders were broad and his stance radiated a determination she found more than compelling. This was a man you could lean on, a man who could take care of the bad guys, wrangle the cattle, and still sweep you off your feet.

"Ethan, aren't you going to say hello to your fiancee?" One of the other men stuck out his hand. "I'm Rob Matheson. This is Cab Johnson and Jamie Lassiter. Ethan here needed some backup."

Rob was blonde, about Ethan's size, but not nearly so serious. In fact, she bet he was a real cut-up. That shit-eating grin probably never left his face. Cab was larger than the others—six foot four maybe, powerfully built. He wore a sheriff's uniform. Jamie was lean but muscular, with dark brown hair that fell into his eyes. They had the easy camaraderie that spoke of a long acquaintance. They probably knew each other as kids, and would take turns being best man at each other's weddings.

Her wedding.

No—she'd be long gone before the month was up. She had three weeks to turn in the story; maybe four, if it was really juicy. She'd pitched it to the editor of CityPretty as soon as the idea occurred to her. Margaret's uncertain approval told her she was probably allowing her one last hurrah before CityPretty let her go.

Still, just for one moment she imagined herself standing side by side Ethan at the altar of some country church, pledging her love to him. What would it be like to marry a near stranger and try to forge a life with him?

Insane, that's what.

So why did the idea send tendrils of warmth into all the right places?

She glanced up at Ethan to find him glancing down, and the warm feeling curved around her insides again. Surely New York men couldn't be shorter than this crew, or any less manly, but she couldn't remember the last time she'd been around so much blatant testosterone. She must be ovulating. Why else would she react like this to a perfect stranger?

Ethan touched her arm. "This way." She followed him down the hall, the others falling into place behind them like a cowboy entourage. She stifled a sudden laugh at the absurdity of it all, slipped her hand into her purse and grabbed her digital camera, capturing the scene with a few clicks. Had this man—this…*cowboy*—sat down and planned out the video he'd made? She tried to picture Ethan bending over a desk and carefully writing out "Sweet. Good cook. Ready for children."

She blew out a breath and wondered if she was the only one stifling in this sudden heat. Ready for children? Hardly. Still…if she was going to make babies with anyone…

Shaking her head to dispel that dangerous image, she found herself at the airport's single baggage carousel. It was just shuddering to life and within moments she pointed out first one, then another sleek, black suitcase. Ethan took them both, began to move toward the door and then faltered to a stop. He avoided her gaze, focusing on something far beyond her shoulder. "It's just…I wasn't…."

Oh God, Autumn thought, a sudden chill racing down her spine. Her stomach lurched and she raised a hand as if to ward off his words. She hadn't even considered this.

He'd taken one look and decided to send her back.

ETHAN STARED INTO THE STRICKEN EYES of the most beautiful woman he'd ever met. He had to confess to her right now the extent of the joke she'd been led into thinking was real. It'd been bad enough when he thought Rob and the rest of them had simply hauled him to the airport for a chance to laugh their asses off at him, but now there was a woman involved, a real, beautiful, fragile woman. He had to stop this before it went any further.

When she raised her clear blue gaze to his, he saw panic, horror, and an awful recognition he instantly realized meant she thought she'd been judged and found wanting. He knew he'd do anything to make that look go away. Judged wanting. As if. The girl was as beautiful as a harvest moon shining on frost-flecked fields in late November. He itched to touch her, take her hand, pull her hard against him and…

Whoa—that thought couldn't go any farther.

He swallowed hard and tried again. "I…it's just my place…something came up and I didn't get a chance to fix it like I meant to." She relaxed a fraction and he rushed on. "It's a good house—built by my great granddaddy in 1889 for the hired help. Solid. Just needs a little attention."

"A woman's touch," Rob threw in.

Ethan restrained himself, barely. He'd get back at all of his friends soon enough. "I just hope you'll be comfortable."

A snigger behind him made him clench his fists.

"I don't mind if it's rough," Autumn said, eliciting a bark of laughter from the peanut gallery. She blushed and Ethan couldn't take his eyes off her face, although he wished she hadn't caught the joke. She'd look like that in bed, after…

Enough.

"Give me the keys," he said to Rob. When his friend hesitated, he held out a hand. "Now."

Rob handed them over with a raised eyebrow, but Ethan just led the way outside and threw Autumn's suitcases in the bed of the truck. He opened the passenger side door.

"Thank you," she said, putting first one foot, then the other on the running board and scrambling somewhat ungracefully into the seat. City girl. At least her hesitation gave him a long moment to enjoy the view.

Rob made as if to open the door to the back bench seat, but Ethan shoved him aside, pressed down the lock and closed the passenger door. He was halfway around the truck before Rob could react.

"Hey, what are you doing?"

"Taking a ride with my fiancee. You all find your own way home." He was in the driver's side with the ignition turning over before any of them moved a muscle. Stupid fools. They'd made their beds and they could sleep in them.

He glanced at the ethereal princess sitting less than

two feet away. Meanwhile, he'd sleep in his own comfortable bed tonight. Maybe with a little company for once.

The Cowboy's E-mail Order Bride (Volume 1)

ABOUT THE AUTHOR

Cora Seton loves cowboys, country life, gardening, bike-riding, and lazing around with a good book. Mother of four, wife to a computer programmer/eco-farmer, she ditched her California lifestyle eight years ago and moved to a remote logging town in northwestern British Columbia.

Like the characters in her novels, Cora enjoys old-fashioned pursuits and modern technology, spending mornings transforming a neglected one-acre lot into a paradise of orchards, berry bushes and market gardens, and afternoons writing the latest Chance Creek romance novel on her iPad mini.

Visit http://www.coraseton.com to read about new releases, locate your favorite characters on the Chance Creek map, and learn about contests and other cool events!